The Coup against Trump
The Story of the Last Days of Donald Trump

AF486130

Introduction

The following is a work of political fiction, a satire about a dystopian very near future, and while including real-life persons is simply a work of speculative fiction. Hopefully by the time you read this book the time period covered in this book will have already passed without any of these events having come true, but if however this book proves to be prophetic, then Zeus help us all because I'm probably already in a concentration camp.

1

September 2020, Virginia.

Hillary's eyes filled with tears as she turned on the television to see the coverage of the death of Ruth Bader Ginsburg. This was exactly what she had feared. She had been hoping against hope that Ruth Bader Ginsburg would be able to hold on until 2021 and then once Biden was in office she could retire and they could replace her with a person who was worthy of the ideals that she stood for.

Hillary shook her head. "Her body isn't even cold and already the Republicans are saying that they are going to replace her, and most likely with a person who goes against everything that she stood for, despite the fact that they said that they wouldn't do this in an election year, hypocrites, all of them!"

"This is God's judgment on America," her brother Brock said. "God killed Justice Ginsburg because she spent her entire life promoting abortion and all sorts of crazy things like feminism. God killed her to make sure that Donald Trump would have no obstacles to the Supreme Court making sure that he becomes president again in 2021."

"Some loving God that you worship, your God sounds more like a hitman than anything," Hillary said confronting her brother. "And you talk a lot about God for a person I have never seen go to church."

"Well at least I believe in God, you're a fucking atheist, you're going to go to hell, just like Ruth Bader Ginsburg."

"Well if that's where she is then it must be a place for the better people, so I would gladly go to hell if people like you are going to be in heaven."

"Children watch your language," said their father Paul. "Sure we have political differences but that doesn't mean we have to curse at one another. But we should see that every cloud has a silver lining. With the death of Justice Ginsburg we can finally get a conservative majority on the Supreme Court like we have been hoping for generations."

"How was I ever born into this family," Hillary said shaking her head.

Hillary's mother Jessica sort of rolled her eyes. She tried to stay out of politics most of the time because it always got really ugly, but in the last few years things had just gotten out of hand where Hillary and Brock could barely even stand the sight of each other, and it made her sad. It went beyond the normal brother and sister rivalry and was to the point where they couldn't even exchange cordial glances at each other. Pretty much every time they talked for more than five minutes it erupted into some type of battlefield.

"You are just still bitter because Hillary didn't win the election, get over it already," Brock said. "You probably only voted for her because you have the same name. God it is such a shameful thing that you have the same name as the worst politician in American history, the stupid bitch."

"Language!" Jessica shouted. "Hillary is going to be going to college soon so you won't have to live together for much longer, so can you just try to treat each other like human beings?"

"Why don't you ask him, he obviously doesn't think the majority of people in this country even deserve human rights or are even considered human," Hillary said. "How many Trump rallies have you been to Brock? How many Mexicans and Blacks have you harassed? You're a freaking Nazi!"

"But hey just because I support Trump doesn't mean that I'm a Nazi," Brock said. "I just don't want this country being ruined by illegals and these BlackLivesMatter terrorists. We should really lock them all up, they are anarchists and terrorists. Look at our whole country, the whole country is in anarchy. That's why I want to be a police officer or maybe become an INS agent."

"Says the juvenile delinquent," Hillary said as they continued yelling at each other.

Jessica shook her head. She felt so sad that her children couldn't get along. When Hillary was younger she used to look up to her brother but they had drifted apart in the last couple of years. Hillary started pursuing her education in hopes of going into civil rights law in college, but Brock just never applied himself academically and had started to get involved with criminal elements.

What Jessica refused to believe is that Brock was one of those alt right extremists. Hillary could see it very clearly. She knew that her brother had clear issues with women and people of color, and she knew that he went around harassing people on the Internet, even though she couldn't prove it because he used so many different aliases. That was where they really started to become heated enemies.

"Hey I may not be perfect but at least I'm not going to college to defend all of these criminals that have taken over the country, the real criminals, the Mexicans who are responsible for all the drugs and rape," Brock said.

"Do you have a single opinion it isn't a direct quote from Donald Trump?" Hillary asked.

"You better watch what you say about Donald Trump, someday he's going to be president for life," Brock said smiling. "12 more years I say."

"You know the Constitution still exists and hasn't been invalidated yet," Hillary said shaking her head. "Honestly you are the reason that people like Hitler come to power. How you can think that somebody like Donald Trump is the second coming of Jesus is beyond me as he goes against everything that Jesus stood for."

"Says the atheist, what do you know about Jesus?"

"Well like most atheists I know a whole lot more about religion and the Bible than most religious believers, which is exactly why I am not a believer. But I do believe in some of the good things that Jesus said. Just because I'm an atheist doesn't mean that I hate

Jesus. If anything the conservative Christians who preach hate all the time, they are the ones who really hate Jesus. The most Christlike people are the unbelievers."

"Well you'll see what God says about that when he condemns you to hell."

"Look I don't need to sit here and listen to another lecture by you with all your alt right Nazi propaganda, I actually have friends who aren't criminals and Nazis and I am going to go see them," Hillary said as she put on her mask.

Brock shook his head. "Putting on your stupid ass mask too, you totally bought into the whole myth of the coronavirus. You know that whole thing is just made up by liberals like you as a way of making Donald Trump look bad. Masks are so gay."

"I guess you had to get in some homophobia too cause you are so secure in your masculinity wearing a mask is enough to make you question your fragile sexuality."

Hillary flipped off Brock as she walked towards the door. Hillary walked a few blocks until she was at her friend Samantha's house. As soon as she opened the door Samantha hugged her.

"I just heard the news about Justice Ginsburg," Samantha said. "I know that she was your hero and the reason why you wanted to study law. So how is your family doing? Somehow I feel like your brother is probably not as broken up about it as you are. How is Brock anyway?"

Hillary put her finger under her nose making a little Hitler mustache before she clacked her heels together and did a Nazi salute, causing Samantha to laugh.

"It is so sad, I used to get along so great with Brock, but in the last few years he has totally become an asshole," Hillary said shaking her head. "I think he's just bitter because no girls want to go out with him. You know he is one of those incel types, sexually frustrated, and takes it out by hating all women. We started to drift apart as soon as he hit puberty but after Donald Trump came onto the scene he had pretty much found a new hero and a new God. Now he wants to become a police officer or an INS agent just so he can brutalize the Mexicans and the Blacks. He has become totally radicalized."

"So does he literally believe that Donald Trump is God or just God's representative on earth? How does anyone buy into that bullshit? I bet he supports every conspiracy theory that Donald Trump spouts doesn't he?"

"Let's put it this way, yesterday I ordered some pizza and he asked me if I got that from the pedophiles at my Democrat meeting."

Samantha rolled her eyes. "Good Lord, the fact that something like that can go mainstream just proves how high the stakes are in this election. And it's really the most absurd conspiracy theory in the world, because if there was some type of child sex trafficking pedophile ring drinking the blood of children to stay young forever you know that Donald Trump would more likely be the head of that operation, rather than the only one opposing it."

"I just can't believe it only took us a few years to go from a world where things seemed to be getting better and now all the sudden we live in a world where racism has basically been revitalized and where truth, fact and objective reality are now meaningless. I really think that they should excavate George Orwell's grave to see if he has turned over in it yet."

"My parents are liberals but largely apolitical and they say that I'm definitely panicking prematurely, they say that there is no way that Donald Trump is going to become dictator, but they just don't realize the fact that a lot of people do want him to become dictator. I mean he jokes about things like creating an executive order to ban Biden from being president or throwing out ballots or chanting 12 more years or president for life, but there are a large number of people who do want him to be president for life. And if I hear one more person say that they think that Donald Trump is the second coming of Jesus or how Christlike the serial rapist is I am probably going to vomit."

"That's why we have to get as many people registered to vote as possible. The stakes of this election couldn't be higher, and if we lose this election or we win this election and allow the results to be overturned that's pretty much the effective end of democracy. What a lot of people don't realize, including a lot of liberals, is how easy it was for people like the Nazis to become democratically elected and then just destroy all democratic institutions."

"Well at least Hitler was actually elected by the popular vote. Just think without the stupid Electoral College we wouldn't have George W. Bush or Donald Trump, pretty much all of the problems of the past 20 years we can directly attribute to the Electoral College. In fact I think that one of the first things that we should do is if we can get the majority needed we should abolish the electoral college and add a couple of new Supreme Court justices."

"Hey I always wanted to be a Supreme Court justice; the more of them there are the better the chances. The problem is if the Republicans get a majority they can stack the court as well and it will just become a never ending Supreme Court arms race."

"Let's just hope that we can get rid of Donald Trump and that his insanity will fade into the past and maybe then we can have an actual democracy that is really representative. Another four years of Donald Trump and I don't think this country is actually going to survive. I really am afraid that we could see a dictatorship. I mean did you see Donald Trump Supreme Court pick, that's actually one of the women who inspired The Handmaid's Tale!"

"Honestly if Donald Trump wins this election, or if he steals this election, I think I want to leave the country," Samantha said shaking her head. "I don't mean that jokingly either. I certainly don't want to be barefoot and pregnant. I'm very very frightened about what this election is going to mean for the country. Even if we win the election who knows if Donald Trump is going to leave office? He's already indicated that he's not going to leave office and that he's going to declare the results of the election invalid if he loses. I don't think that people are really taking this seriously enough and realizing that legitimate threat that he proposes to the continuation of American democracy. In fact if people hadn't been so lazy about having uncritical faith in the democratic institutions we wouldn't be seeing them challenged right now. We could very well lose everything."

Hillary nodded. "But we have to stay positive; we have to assume that the rule of law will prevail. And if it comes down to it we have to hope that the military will restore the Constitution and remove Donald Trump from orifice by force if he won't leave willingly."

The two of them stood there but neither of them could say with full confidence that that would necessarily be the case. But they didn't want to contemplate this anymore so they decided to get to work and go ahead and register as many people to vote as they could.

"Let's get started," Samantha said.

2

October 31, 2020.

"I hope you liberals are happy," Brock said shaking his head. "You've used your stupid coronavirus hoax to effectively cancel Halloween."

"As a Christian don't you think that Halloween is just Satanism anyway," Hillary said. "Besides who needs Halloween, with people supporting Donald Trump there is enough horror in this country already."

Brock shook his head. "The real horror is the fact that our country is overrun with illegals and BlackLivesMatter protesters and all sorts of other terrorists. You won't think it's so funny if you get raped by a bunch of Mexicans. Let's see how much you want to defend the illegals after they have gone sex trafficking you all the way to Mexico. Just be glad that there are people like me who still believe in this country and want to stand up for the founding ideals of this country."

Hillary knew that it was pointless to argue with Brock. The last month had been a pure living hell between them where they could barely even look at each other without wanting to scream. The election had continued to grow more heated by the day, and she was glad that in another week or so it would be over one way or the other.

Hillary began putting on her mask.

"Where are you going, to see your stupid lesbian friend," Brock said.

"Samantha is not a lesbian, she's pansexual," Hillary said underneath her mask.

"What's that, like a hobbit or something?" Brock asked. "She didn't want to go out with me so I figure that she was kind of a lesbian. Every time I sort of make the moves on her she moves away in disgust."

"Samantha is not a lesbian, she just as something called standards Brock. You know that not every woman who doesn't want to go out with you is a lesbian; there just aren't that many lesbians in the population. Maybe if you didn't think every woman was a bitch or a hoe or if you treated them with respect they would actually want to go out with you. Anyway I have lots of things to do."

"You mean spreading communist propaganda?"

"Yeah we are totally coming for your guns, so you had better sleep closely with them," Hillary said shaking her head and rolling her eyes.

Hillary held up a Biden Harris sign and stuck out her tongue at him as she walked out the door to go see Samantha.

"I guess this is our last final drive to try and get people to see reason," Samantha said as they went out to hand out bumper stickers.

"My brother thinks that you're a lesbian because you don't want to go out with him," Hillary said with a laugh.

"Hey I would take any woman who respects me as a human being over any man who doesn't," Samantha said. "In fact if you're still single I could use a date for this weekend."

Hillary hugged Samantha. "I'm flattered but I have to admit I'm still totally heterosexual."

"You don't know what you're missing."

"Hey I know most men are jerks, but there are some good men out there, I can't help the way God made me," Hillary said as they both burst out laughing. "What can I say, I just like the idea of having a Dick inside of me."

The two of them began laughing as they started walking up and down the streets. They saw that the streets were notably absent of trick-or-treaters, and they found that they got a hostile reception because during a pandemic people didn't want to see trick-or-treaters, but in this part of the country they didn't really want to see people going around campaigning either.

"I have to admit it is a little bit sad that Halloween was canceled," Hillary said. "Brock thinks that Halloween was canceled because of some type of a liberal plot against trick-or-treaters. Yes he really does believe that."

Samantha shook her head. "I will never understand the mind of a conspiracy theorist. Look I don't deny that sometimes conspiracies happen, like with Watergate, but there are rational conspiracies and then there are like 95% of conspiracies which are just the delusions of bunch of right-wing people paranoid about everything that progressives, women or people of color do."

The two of them continued walking feeling that they should probably be getting home soon. They figured that they were fighting a losing battle in their part of the country as their town was very firmly Trump territory. In fact as they walked up street after street seeing sign after sign with Trump 2020 on it, it was admittedly rather disheartening and depressing.

As they were getting ready to go home that was when they saw what looked like a rally taking place in the center of town.

"What do you think is going on there?" Samantha said as she pointed in the direction of the rally.

"I don't know, do you think we should go check it out?" Hillary asked.

Samantha shrugged her shoulders as the two of them walked towards the center of town where it looked like there was a rally being held in favor of Trump, with all people holding up Trump signs and lots of Confederate flags and swastikas as well.

"Maybe we should get out of here as I don't think that this is a place that will probably be very welcoming for what we are selling," Samantha said.

"Yeah this is more of Brock's type of crowd unfortunately," Hillary said and that was when she noticed someone at the head of the crowd holding a bullhorn that looked distinctly familiar.

"These liberals, they're coming for our guns, they're coming for our freedoms, they're going to make us all wear masks and try to get us all vaccinated because of this coronavirus hoax," Brock said to his bullhorn. "Liberals are the reasons why your children can't walk the street safely on Halloween tonight. Liberals are the reason why our country is in anarchy and why our cities are filled with rioters and chaos. The Blacks and the Mexicans and the minorities have taken over this country, but in a couple of days we are going to take this country back from the people who have taken it from real God-fearing Americans. They say that we are the hatemongers, but they just hate our freedoms, they hate our numbers. We are the silent majority, but we will not stay silent any longer."

Hillary shook her head. "If you are the 'silent' majority why are you shouting from a bullhorn," she said as she elbowed Samantha.

"That brother of yours is a real piece of work isn't he," Samantha said rolling her eyes.

"We need to send a message this election day that we are not going to take the liberals and all of their politically correct bullshit anymore," Brock continued as the people in the crowd held up torches. "We are not going to let transgender perverts invade our bathrooms. We are not going to allow abortionists murder our white Christian babies. We are not going to allow these BlackLivesMatter and antifa terrorists destroy our heritage and our monuments and make our city streets full of anarchy and chaos. We are not going to allow illegals to take all of our welfare money. We are not going to allow liberals to use all of their phony scientific theories about coronavirus and climate change as a way of restricting our freedoms and undermining the God-given authority of our president who was sent here by God himself to save America from the lunatics who are trying to take it away from us. That is why I want you all to go out there and intimidate a liberal. If liberals think that their votes are going to count they should think again. I want all of you to try and convince liberals not to vote. And if you know anyone who is against our president Trump I want you to start keeping tabs on them. I think that we all know that he is not going to leave office no matter what this phony baloney election says. We know that the only way he can lose is if the election is rigged, and if the election is rigged the only thing we can do, the only patriotic thing to do, is to reject the results of the election if it doesn't turn out the way God intended with a victory for our grand leader Donald Trump. Now I want us to go through the town and let them know that we aren't going to take it anymore. We are fed up, we are pissed off and we are not going to take this liberal bullshit anymore."

Everyone in the crowd began cheering and waving

noisemakers and holding up torches.

"I think your brother is about to incite a riot," Samantha said. "I think maybe we should get out of here."

Hillary nodded. "I'm with you."

"Hey look it's a bunch of those masked communists who are trying to take away our freedoms," someone in the crowd shouted pointing at Hillary and Samantha who were wearing their Biden Harris T-shirts.

As Hillary stood there she could see that Brock was making direct eye contact with her. She was hoping that her brother would say something and try to get control of the crowd and the riot that he seemed to be inciting. She was hoping that her brother would still have some shred of human decency and sense of familial loyalty to his very own sister. But as he stood there saying nothing she knew that blood was certainly not thicker than water in this case.

"Let's get the hell out of here," Samantha said as the two of them began running as the rioters that Brock had incited began shouting and marching through the streets. She could see that they were ripping up the signs on people's lawns that said Biden Harris on them and they knew that it wasn't safe for them to be in town.

Samantha and Hillary ran all the way home and Samantha told Hillary to call her the second she got home to make sure she got home safely.

Hillary walked into the house where she could see her parents watching the television.

"And now we have a cure for the so-called coronavirus, and remember it was delivered to you by my administration," Donald Trump said on television. "Remember that when you go to vote this Tuesday."

Hillary was practically out of breath as her parents turned around to see her.

"Hillary is something the matter?" Jessica asked. "You look like something is troubling you. Also do you have any idea where your brother went? He sort of left the house without telling us where he was going again and we are worried that he might be getting up to some type of Halloween mischief. Remember last year when he went around silly stringing all of those houses and throwing toilet paper and eggs all over the place? I really don't want him coming home in a police car again."

Hillary knew she should say something. In fact she didn't know why she didn't say something considering the way her brother had just treated her. But to her maybe family still meant something and maybe blood was thicker than water. If Brock was going to get himself arrested she didn't want to be the one to be the bearer of bad news, so she decided to play ignorant.

Hillary shrugged her shoulders. "Like I would even care where that guy is, he's probably off with a bunch of his lowlife friends. Anyway I told Samantha that I would call her when I got home."

"Okay but don't stay up too late dear," Jessica said as they went back to watching the news.

"I got home safely," Hillary said on the phone.

"What about Brock?" Samantha asked.

Hillary shook her head. "I don't know what he is up to right now, but I am sure that he's up to no good. I didn't want to be the one to break the news to my parents, and personally I don't care if he does come home in a police car at this point. After the way he treated us today, after the fact that his lynch mob nearly killed us, he can just go fuck himself."

But as Hillary put down the phone and prepared to go to bed she found that she would not sleep easy that night as she was thinking about her brother, and even though she knew that she shouldn't, she somehow still felt worried about him.

"I guess we will see what the morning brings," Hillary said as she closed her eyes and went to sleep.

3

November 3, 2020, Election Day.

Hillary woke up bright and early that morning setting her alarm so that she could get to the polling places as quickly as possible. She had agreed that she and Samantha would go to the polls and vote together in their first election in which they were looking forward to vote in what they hoped wouldn't be the last election in American history. She also was planning to meet up there with her boyfriend Jordan who felt this election would determine whether or not he would be able to safely walk the streets free of police intimidation. As an active member of BlackLivesMatter he felt that this would probably be the most important election of his life, and few people disagreed with him on that.

As the three of them got in line for voting they could see that the lines were rather long and that they would probably be there for a while.

"I'm just glad that I didn't drink too much because I certainly wouldn't want to have to leave the line to go to the bathroom," Samantha said shaking her head. "I don't know if we should consider this voter turnout to be encouraging or discouraging. On the one hand I am glad to see that a lot of people are coming out to vote, but seeing as we live in a county that has gone for Trump in the last election it may not be a good thing that large numbers of people from our town are voting."

Hillary looked around and she could see at least a couple of other people who were wearing T-shirts like them with Biden Harris on it, which made her feel a little bit encouraged that at least not everyone in her town was a crazed racist Trump supporter. But she had to admit it looked like they were the minority in that crowd, as she saw a lot more people who seemed to be enthusiastic fascists.

Hillary smiled as she looked at some of the other women in line and turned to Samantha. "Well I suppose we did everything we can and now we just have to do the last thing and do the voting, and hopefully things will turn out in our favor."

"Yeah but remember last time when we all thought that Hillary had the thing in the bag and we never in a million years thought that this maniac would win," Samantha said. "This year I didn't plan a party the way I did four years ago."

Hillary remembered that really depressing day where they had stayed up all night with lots of their friends to watch the election results, pretty much assured of a Hillary Clinton victory where they were going to party and celebrate the election of our first female president. As the night wore on their pessimism turned to despair and they ended up crying themselves to sleep that night.

Hillary shook her head. "That was a rather depressing party if there ever was one. But hey let's keep optimistic and hope that everything turns out all right this time. Maybe we aren't going to prematurely plan a party like we did last time, but if things turn out well we can have a party to celebrate the end of American fascism."

Jordan shook his head. "Even if Donald Trump goes away his hateful ideology is not going to go away easily. The fact is for African-Americans like myself we have always been living under fascism. Things have just gotten so bad in the last couple of years that now even white people are recognizing it. I'm not talking about you, you were both always woke as hell and that's what I love about you, but I think if we have learned anything from the last four years it is just how easy the winds of change can shift in a direction that is unfavorable."

"Yeah but I don't want to get down about this until we have to feel bad about it," Hillary said. "I'm not going to get myself all worked up for nothing. I want to see the results of this election before I decide whether to celebrate or whether I'm going to have to be placed on suicide watch."

"Hey don't even joke about that," Jordan said. "But I fully understand how you feel, but after everything that has happened in the last four years I am extremely pessimistic. If people were logical and rational and tolerant Donald Trump would've never even had a chance to be a viable candidate, the fact that he actually got into power in the first place should be enough to terrify all of us about the future of this country. And even if we do completely win in a landslide in this election we still have to get him out of office. He has even said that he's not necessarily going to accept the results of the election if he loses."

"I know but the Constitution says that he has to leave office," Samantha said.

Hillary shook her head. "Yes but you know as well as I do that dictators don't play by the rules. Even if we win this election fair and square we know that tyrants like Donald Trump have a million tricks up their sleeves to find some way to keep themselves in power. Lots of Third World countries started out as democracies and then the leaders just overturned the election results. Four years ago people would have never said that that was possible in America, but now we have the president directly saying pretty much that he wants to be a dictator and that hasn't been enough to cause people to rise up."

"One of the problems is that all of the people who say that we need to second amendment to safeguard the Constitution against the rise of a dictatorship are unfortunately the racists who are in favor of fascism," Jordan said. "Let's face it, if this is going to result in a civil war or some type of military junta unfortunately the people in support of that are at the greater advantage. As liberals of course we support gun control because that's the sane and rational thing, but sanity and rationality can't stand up to people who are better armed than we are. That is why although I oppose the NRA I still support the right to bear arms. If a war is going to start I am going to go down fighting."

"Okay let's just try not to focus on the bad and just try to focus on the issue at hand," Hillary said. "We don't know what's going to happen after the election, but right now it's important that we make sure that the election at least takes place. The more overwhelming the victory for Biden the harder it will be for the Supreme Court and the other corrupted institutions of our democracy to help Donald Trump to remain in power. The more obvious it is to the American people that Biden won fairly and squarely the easier it will be to convince people to not let the country be taken over by a dictatorship."

Jordan nodded his head. "But like we already said, dictators don't play by the rules. As terrible as the worst case scenario is it is possible that winning an election doesn't necessarily mean we are going to remove the tyrant from office or have a peaceful transition of power. Personally I don't trust him, and for good reason. No matter what the results of this election are things are going to get ugly and they are going to get ugly fast."

"Look at the stupid nigger and his two bitches wearing masks," some guy said as he walked past.

"Well I guess we know who he is voting for," Samantha said. "This is exactly why there should be some type of intelligence test that you have to take in order to qualify to vote."

"I can't believe you're going to let him get away with that,"

Hillary said. "He racially slurred you."

"But the best revenge we can get on people like that is voting against them," Jordan said. "Although I did feel even angrier when he called you two bitches."

Hillary admired Jordan's ability to stay calm, cool and collected under the circumstances. But he has been called a lot worse and been treated a lot worse by racists, so he knew that you have to choose your battles. Growing up as an African-American in a mostly white town with a strong racist contingent you don't want to challenge the status quo too directly. People of color in this country just had to tow a fine line so that they wouldn't find themselves being attacked physically by responding to a verbal assault.

"I just know I don't want to be the next George Floyd or Trayvon Martin," Jordan said. "I don't want to become a statistic on the news that people protest around. I want to live to see the world get better."

The three of them looked at a bunch of people on the sidelines; some of them holding up signs that said beware the New World order, challenge the deep state, stuff about pizza gate and a whole lot of other things, most of which were equally idiotic and paranoid.

One guy came over with a bullhorn making all sorts of pronouncements to the people in line. "Masks cannot silence us. We all know that this whole entire pandemic was just a way to try and make Donald Trump lose the election and that it's a plot by Bill Gates to get people to accept the chip, but we are not going to be vaccinated and not be a slave to the United Nations and the New World order."

As he put down his bullhorn he started doing something on his phone and Samantha looked at him and shook her head.

"Hey idiot, if you have a smartphone you are already basically being tracked and monitored everywhere you go, probably by Russians, so I wouldn't worry so much about being vaccinated and getting chipped," Samantha said. "If you are using social media and an Internet device you are probably already being mined for data by people all around the world. Trust me if there is some evil cabal of people trying to take over the world you have already played easily into their hands."

"But that's just what they want you to think!" he said. "We all know the Bill Gates and George Soros are part of some type of global conspiracy to enslave the world. This whole coronavirus hoax, it was just a way to get us to wear masks. In fact wearing masks is an easier way to get infected. Then they will come forward with a miracle cure and that is how they will get everyone to take it. They will force them to take it just like they forced all those children to be vaccinated to give them autism. It's all part of a plot to take over the world. This whole election thing is just a sham and you're an idiot for believing in it."

Samantha wanted to argue with him, but she didn't want to argue with idiots, that was never a productive use of her time, although the last thing that he said made her feel uneasy because in the pit of her stomach she felt like that last part might turn out to be true. Until the election was over and all decided she couldn't be perfectly sure that it was going to actually be a legitimate election and that they weren't going to wake up some day to a dictatorship. The way she felt was that people didn't have to plot to take over the world in secret, the lunatics had already conquered the world right under everybody's noses, and with few standing up to it.

Hillary shook her head and started waving her finger around her ears indicating that she thought that the man with the bullhorn was crazy as Jordan and Samantha nodded and repeated the gesture back to her.

As Hillary looked at the guy with the bullhorn going around spouting conspiracy theory bullshit she couldn't help but think of her brother. Neither of them had spoken since the incident on Halloween and he didn't come home that night in a police car the way she was expecting. She never said anything to her parents either. She didn't like to be a snitch, even on a total bastard like her brother.

She did hear about reports of vandalism throughout the town but she figured that the police probably had a black man to harass or something like that, so her brother wasn't caught. But she figured even if her brother did get caught he would probably get a slap on the wrist or community service at best, but inciting a riot, that was something that she could see on his criminal history sheet someday.

Her brother didn't say anything about going to vote for the election or anything like that and she didn't even see him that morning. She was kind of wondering where he was at the moment, because for someone who is such an enthusiastic supporter it didn't seem like he was showing up to vote. Of course given who he was going to vote for she felt that was probably a good thing.

However she also thought about all of the possibilities of everything that could go wrong with the election, and she was wondering if her brother was off with all of his criminal friends perhaps plotting some type of demonstration if the election did not go well. She just didn't know exactly what he was capable of after that last night, and it was not a thought that put her mind at ease.

Finally it was time for them to vote and when Jordan went up to show his ID he was turned away.

"This is bullshit, I was totally registered to vote," Jordan said. "And I don't have any type of criminal history or fines to pay off or anything like that either."

"Is there a problem here," a security officer said as he came over to Jordan.

Jordan was furious but once again he knew when to pick his battles. He knew that he had a right to vote but he expected that something like this was going to happen.

"No officer, there is no problem," Jordan said. "Just the fact that my democratic right has been taken away from and I have been disenfranchised by the United States of America. But I'm black, so I guess I have to get used to it don't I?"

"Are you giving me lip boy?" the security agent said.

Hillary and Samantha wanted to say something but they knew that Jordan didn't want to rock the boat and find himself arrested. They were both furious to see this display of obvious racism and disenfranchisement, but they also were sad to say that they weren't surprised.

"I guess I should have voted by mail," Jordan said. "But I felt it was better to actually show up hoping that my vote would actually be counted."

"If you're not going to vote I will have to ask you to leave," the security agent said as he started browbeating Jordan.

"Well I waited to vote but I guess it looks like I'm not going to now am I," Jordan said as he looked to Samantha and Hillary. "Well you ladies make your vote count for me since I have been disenfranchised."

Hillary hugged and kissed Jordan and looked at him in the eye. "Don't worry we will win this thing for you and we will see you later tonight."

Later that evening they all gathered at Hillary's house to watch the election result, all of them with their fingers crossed and praying.

"I thought you were an atheist," Jordan said.

"Yeah I am, so that should really be telling you something," Hillary said as she laughed. "I'm also wearing a lucky rabbit's foot. I still can't believe what happened to you today as that is a total injustice. Your first election and they didn't even allow you to vote. You should find some way to legally challenge it or something like that. This is exactly why I wanted to become a civil rights attorney, to protect those people like you who have done nothing wrong and find themselves being persecuted by the state."

"Holy shit Texas went blue," Samantha said. "I can't believe that, this is definitely a miracle. Are you sure that there is no God Hillary? I'm starting to think that maybe she is on our side this time."

"Let's just hope that it stays blue," Jordan said. "If we can actually flip Texas to be blue I think we can prevent another Republican president from ever happening again."

Hillary smiled. "If we've got Texas I think that we've got this thing. There's no way Donald Trump could even have a chance if he couldn't win Texas. I don't want to get prematurely optimistic but I am feeling a lot better right now."

"They just called Virginia for Biden!" Samantha shouted as the three of them high-fived each other.

"You know I don't like to get ahead of myself and everything, but I can't help but thinking that we had a little bit of something to do with that," Hillary said as they smiled and laughed.

"Well we did our part anyway, and it looks like it's paying off," Samantha said. "I think that Americans are finally loudly and boldly declaring that they reject fascism and hatred. We aren't going to take this shit anymore."

Jordan smiled as well. "He may not be Bernie Sanders, but I have never been more relieved to see who is going to be our next president."

They continued watching and getting exciting as state after state was flipped blue.

"I think that we're actually going to flip the Senate, which is what we need to undo all the damage that Trump has done," Samantha said. "To win the presidency but not to win a majority is pretty much the same as hardly winning at all. But I have to admit I am feeling pretty good right now. And if we get a majority in the Senate I think it's about time we had a couple of new Supreme Court justices to take back the ones that Donald Trump stole from Obama and from the people."

"It looks like they are calling the election for Biden," Jordan said. "I think with his landslide like this, with a blue wave, let's say a blue tsunami even, I don't even think Fox news is going to be able to deny the results of this election now."

"It looks like they are going to Trump headquarters to see if he is going to concede," Hillary said. "Somehow I doubt that he's going to concede graciously."

The three of them watched the TV carefully as they went to collect a statement from Donald Trump.

"The results of this election are invalid and I will not concede to a rigged election," Donald Trump said. "I will take this to every court in America if it is necessary. Just look at the numbers, do any of you out there really believe that Biden won by that huge of a margin? The reports that he won are fake news. Do you think Americans would really vote for anarchy and the chaos of the last several months of the last year? I am the only one who can save America and I am not going to give up so easily, and I will not let the American people be cheated out of the real results of the election. Prepare for a legal battle."

They changed the channel to Fox News where they were reporting that the president had the election stolen from him and will challenge the thieves in court.

As the three of them stared at the TV and looked at each other they could already see that things had gotten as ugly as they thought it would be, and not just because the president looked like an orange turd with a bird's nest on top.

"Tonight you people have effectively killed America," Brock said as he came up behind them, startling them, and from the look that she saw in his eyes she knew that something had changed in him and it was not for the better.

4

"It still seems that Donald Trump is refusing to concede the election to Joe Biden despite the fact that he appears to have a landslide victory," the newscaster said as they went to a clip of Donald Trump.

"Why do I keep contesting the results of the election?" Donald Trump said. "Because it was a rigged election, the Democrats knew that the only way that they could win the election is if they used massive voter fraud such as all of these mail in ballots that I am trying to cease the counting of. The fact is we had lots of people voting, lots of dead people voting, lots of people voting who aren't even citizens of this country. These are the exact type of people that the Democrats want to take over, they want the criminals to vote, they want the illegals to vote and they are just bitter because they want to retake the Supreme Court now that it has a solid conservative majority."

The newscaster continued to cover the continuing election results which every day showed even more in favor of Biden than they did on the original election night. It was true that every time that more mail in ballots were counted that it helped Biden, but as far as most people were concerned Biden clearly won the election on election night itself.

"Now that the Democrats have retaken the Senate the question is are they going to pack the Supreme Court to get back a liberal majority?" one of the newscaster said. "There is a lot at stake with this new presidency, and after Ruth Bader Ginsburg's Supreme Court seat was taken, someone say stolen from the Democrats by Donald Trump, in spite of his own party's insistence that they wouldn't appoint a new Supreme Court justice in an election year, the continuing of Roe V Wade might be completely contingent upon Democrats managing to stack the court with new liberal justices. Conservatives are already scrambling to challenge Roe V Wade in what looks like it will be the final weeks and months of Donald Trump's presidency. And all the while the recounts and the legal challenges to stop the counting of mail in ballots continue."

Hillary turned off the television and shook her head. "When is Donald Trump finally going to face reality and realize that he lost this election and there is nothing he can do legally to challenge that?"

"Donald Trump face reality, his whole presidency was based on ignoring all reality and all science, logic and reason," Samantha said. "And to say nothing of basic human decency, you know he's never going to willingly leave office until he is dragged from office by force."

"Hopefully to some type of guillotine," Hillary said shaking her head. "People like Donald Trump simply don't know how to be told no. He was always a natural dictator and that was always his plan from becoming president. He never wanted to become president; he wanted to become dictator, president for life. He can't stand anyone challenging him, especially people he perceives as lesser than him, which to him is basically everyone. He is a narcissistic egomaniac with delusions of grandeur."

"And his followers are no better," Samantha said shaking her head. "First there was that tragic mass shooting only a few towns over on Election Day. Some of Trump's supporters were so determined to keep black people from voting that they started shooting at people just so that they would close all the polling places. What is this world coming to?"

"And have you seen the protests on TV. I remember when we had all the women's marches against Donald Trump that we participated in and where the conservatives were yelling at us to get over it he's your president. Now that they on the losing side they are basically starting riots throughout America. People are actually calling for Civil War if Donald Trump is not declared the winner of this election."

Hillary shook her head. "If it comes down to that it comes

down to that, but I hope that it won't come down to that. Somehow I feel like Americans aren't really ready for a Civil War. We may hate each other but we are all very lazy and cowardly, and a Civil War takes a lot of real effort."

Samantha nodded. "You do have a point but I think that these riots are not just run-of-the-mill riots, and I think that they are something deeper. We see the Trump supporters are marching in places and marching to courthouses brandishing machine guns. They say that BlackLivesMatter was a violent protest when it was peaceful, and look at them, a total double standard."

"I'm just glad that nothing happened to Jordan. I don't know what would happen if something happened to him, I don't know how I could take that. That mass shooting was just a few counties over, and to think that instead of just losing out on getting to vote the Jordan could have been shot, it makes me sick to my stomach. We actually have Nazis marching in the streets and running over protesters with their cars. These people really mean business."

"Did you see all those burned effigies of Joe Biden? These people are convinced that he is trying to take over the entire world."

"Well to be fair isn't becoming president the same as taking over the world more or less? If that is what it is I say let him take over the world, he won the election fair and square, he should take over so that he can begin cleaning up the mess the Donald Trump has made of this country in the last four years. He will probably spend his entire first term just cleaning up the mess. It seems like every time we have a Republican president it's always the Democrat's job to basically just clean up the mess so that we can get back to square one. It's just getting ridiculous."

"How is Brock taking it?"

"Something really snapped inside of him and I am worried about him. It wasn't just that he nearly incited a riot on Halloween and most likely was responsible for all those acts of vandalism, but now he just sort of stares at the TV all day, almost like he is in a trance. He has Fox News blasting loudly with their proclamations that the American people have to rise up and ensure that Donald Trump stays in power or the country will descend into anarchy. He keeps going on about how we stole the election from Donald Trump and now he's the only one who can save us and protect us from the country being overrun with minorities."

"You don't think you would do something crazy like try to kill Joe Biden, do you?"

Hillary frowned. "I don't even know what he is capable of any more. I know he is still my brother and I would like to believe that there is still good inside of him, but it seems like as time goes on he becomes more and more hateful and radicalized. Supporting Trump has basically become like his religion, the Trump supporters have become something of a cult, and I think they are becoming something of a suicide cult. Did you hear about the mass suicides that took place in protest of –"

"I am just getting sick of hearing all the news. It seemed like we finally had a fair election but it's still tearing the country completely apart. Although I'm not really worried about your brother killing Joe Biden as I think that the Secret Service is probably smarter than your brother."

"Brock always wanted to be a part of the Secret Service, said he has to defend the leader, saying that America is nothing without a strong forceful leader who will take charge and not listen to all of the naysayers."

"So essentially he wants a dictator. I'm afraid that that's what a lot of Americans want, and sometimes I worry that Donald Trump is going to get what he wants after all, like he always has. He's just really not used to getting his own way all the time or listening to anyone. Donald Trump is actively delusional; he lives in a world where he really genuinely believes that he won the election and that every single vote against him was illegal, despite the fact that there is pretty much no voter fraud evidence whatsoever."

"I'm afraid to get pizza after I heard that pizza place being bombed on election night where not more than a few feet away someone spray-painted a giant Q on the wall. I don't want to believe we are going to descend into a Civil War but it looks like it's a very real possibility. In fact it may already have started. When you see the people engaging in having insurrection against the legitimate president and his followers what do you call that? Maybe we are not formally in a state of civil war yet but we are in some type of state of insurrection. I think a lot of people are just going to continue to see Donald Trump as the legitimate president no matter how illegal it is for him to stay in office.

"Like I said, even though we seem to have won the election by a landslide I still think that maybe it would be safer to go to Canada. I don't mean that jokingly, I have been wondering about that for a long time. I have heard that after this election Canada is already strengthening its border security. They figure that a Civil War is a real possibility and that a lot of Americans might try to storm the borders. So maybe a lot of people in America don't believe we are in a state of civil war, but the Canadians seem to think that we do, and I have to say I trust the Canadians more than I trust the Americans."

Hillary frowned again. "And you know if we are in a state of civil war I have no doubt that my brother is likely one of those people would actively fight it. Last night I saw him in his room cleaning his guns, all the while with that same vacant stare on his face. I think that Donald Trump losing the election caused him to lose his mind. I really do think that something is going on with him and it's making me nervous."

Samantha nodded. "You know I know it's not the correct thing to say but sometimes I think that maybe someone should just shoot Donald Trump. Sometimes people have to be removed by force."

"We don't want to resort to the tactics of the other side though, do we? We want to prove that we are nonviolent; we want a peaceful transition of power, not a bloody coup. But sometimes I fear that you are right, Jordan seems to think similar. He doesn't think that Donald Trump is ever going to leave office peacefully or willingly and Donald Trump has said as much himself. Even if the courts decide that his presidency is illegitimate I think that he is going to do everything in his power to try and prevent Joe Biden from taking office. Unfortunately Donald Trump is sort of a force like gravity. For some reason he seems to come across as extremely charismatic to assholes. In fact I think that's why people have been empowered by him, the wrong people, the Nazis and the racists. Donald Trump is basically the person who gave them permission to be their worse, and they have fully taken advantage of it."

As the two of them continued chatting suddenly they heard someone at the door. They opened the door and standing there was their friend Cecelia.

"Hey Cecelia, how have you been?" Samantha asked. "In case you are wondering we haven't decided to have a party yet until Donald Trump finally concedes the election to Joe Biden. We don't want to have another depressing Hillary as president party that ends up becoming bitterly ironic."

Samantha and Hillary smiled but they realized that Cecelia wasn't smiling.

"Is something wrong Cecelia?" Hillary asked. "We are just as nervous about the political situation as anything but we are trying to remain positive that it's all going to work out in the end."

"Who cares about the bloody election?!" Cecelia said tears streaming down her face. This was definitely not normal behavior for her because she was even a more voracious political campaigner than they were. But they hadn't seen her in nearly a week and she didn't even go to vote with them on Election Day.

"Cecelia what is the matter?" Samantha said as they led her into the house and sat her down on the couch.

Cecelia looked at Hillary almost with a look of disgust.

"Did I do something wrong?" Hillary said as Cecelia wiped away her tears with a tissue and shook her head.

"It's nothing that you did wrong, but it concerns someone that you know and I don't know how you are going to take it or whether you're even going to believe me," Cecelia said. "Hillary I want you to know that no matter what I always consider you a close friend and I know that you are nothing like him."

"Like who?" Hillary asked, but immediately somehow she knew as she looked at Cecelia's face as she couldn't even make eye contact with Hillary. Hillary grabbed Cecelia by the chin and lifted her face up until they were eye to eye. "What did Brock do?"

Cecelia broke down and began crying barely able to form words.

"No, he didn't, he couldn't have," Hillary said as she shook her head but she knew right away what had happened. "When did it happen?"

"It happened on Halloween," Cecelia said continuing to wipe away tears and looking like she was about to be sick. "I was just walking down the street when your brother lead what looked like a mob through the town. He came on to me and when I slapped him he smacked me hard across the face and called me a liberal cunt. And then he, then he –"

Now Hillary was the one who was about to be sick. She knew that Brock was a sick individual and a misogynist and an incel, but as much as she hated him, deep down in her heart she didn't want to believe that her brother would actually rape someone. But he always had a thing for Cecelia and had gotten grabby with her in the past but now he had gone too far. Now she realized why exactly Brock had been acting weird the last couple of days, even for him. Apparently it had nothing to do with the election after all, that was just a symptom of a deeper problem.

"I think that I am going to have to have a talk with my brother," Hillary said now fighting back tears.

"No don't," Cecelia said. "I don't want to press charges against him; I just don't want it to happen again. I don't want to send your brother to jail."

"You wouldn't be the first one," Hillary said shaking her head. "Cecelia I believe you, I believe women, and if my brother really did what you say he did and I believe you fully, then I will be the first one to testify against him."

At that moment any feelings of loyalty or familial loyalty that Hillary had to Brock had been completely destroyed and her loyalty was entirely with Cecelia. In fact right then and there she wanted to kill Brock, or castrate him at the very least.

"Cecelia I am going to make sure that justice is done and I'm going to confront Brock right now," Hillary said as she stood up.

"Please don't, I don't want to cause any trouble in your family," Cecelia said as she grabbed Hillary by the arm and pulled her back down to the seat.

Hillary looked her right in the eye. "Cecelia my brother has already caused plenty of trouble in my family and it's all his own fault. I am not going to let him get away with doing this to one of my close friends. Don't even try to stop me, I'll kill him myself if I have to."

"Hillary wait," Samantha said looking terrified. "I am not siding with your brother by any means, but he could be dangerous. I don't want you to confront him alone as he could get violent. I think that we should all go together and we should all bring our pepper spray in case he tries anything."

Hillary, Samantha and Cecelia began walking back to Hillary's house but they could see that as they were approaching it Cecelia was breaking down and couldn't go herself.

"Brock I'm going to kill you," Hillary said as she stormed in through the door to see her parents sitting there looking sad.

"Hillary your brother has run away," Jessica said holding up a note and crying. "I don't know where he is, do you have any idea?"

Hillary wanted to say something to her mother, wanted to say the truth about Brock, but as she looked into her mother's eyes, grieving for the loss of her son who had run away from her, she didn't have the heart to tell her at that moment that her beloved child was a rapist.

So Hillary did the next best thing, the only thing that she could do under the circumstances, and turned to the side and got sick.

5

November 26, 2020, Thanksgiving Day.

"And the wave of riots and protests continues as several cities erupt into chaos of people protesting the results of the election," the newscaster said among scenes of cities with clouds of smoke rising up. "Just days after all of the courts have pronounced that the election results are legitimate and that Joe Biden was the winner Donald Trump still insists that the results are illegitimate, and his followers refuse to accept the results of the election. Democrats are pointing to the hypocrisy of Donald Trump not wanting to impose martial law in cities where protests in favor of him have raged out of control and done millions of dollars in damage. At the same time Donald Trump has been issuing a series of sweeping executive orders calling for the arrest of BlackLivesMatter protesters, antifa members and people believed to be illegal aliens.

The wave of arrests is unprecedented and many feel that Donald Trump is using his executive orders as a way of trying to maintain control of the country which has slipped into chaos in the aftermath of the election."

"This is what you're going to have for the next four years under Biden," Donald Trump said on television. "You're going to have anarchy, you are going to have rioting and disorder and total and utter chaos, and this is precisely why I cannot be allowed to leave office. Is this what you want your nation coming to?"

Hillary turned off the television. "The rioters are the people rioting because they want you in power, this is all because of you, you jackass."

Hillary sat down on the couch. This was going to be her last Thanksgiving at home before she went to college and she had to admit it was a sad one as the entire country had erupted into total chaos. In the last several weeks nobody had heard from her brother Brock, but at this point she didn't even really want to see him. Every time she thought of him or every time she saw his picture also could think about was Cecelia crying at what he had done to her.

The thing that worried her though is that because she didn't know where Brock was she didn't know what he was doing. She wouldn't be surprised if he was among the rioters or that he was in prison somewhere and didn't want to call home. But the other thing that she worried is that if he did that to Cecelia what might he be doing to other women out there?

"I just really wish that your brother was here with us this Thanksgiving," Jessica said as she came out of the kitchen shaking her head.

"Well I don't," Hillary said as she crossed her arms and turned away from her mother.

Jessica shook her head. "I just wish you two could get along. I am worried about your brother, we have no idea where he is and we haven't heard from him in weeks. I know you have had your differences but he is still your brother and he is still a good person. He may not be perfect, but who is?"

Hillary wanted to shout that he was a dirty no good rapist, but as she looked into her mother's eyes, which were full of pleading and looked like they were about to fill with tears again, she knew that she couldn't do that to her. At the same time however she felt that she should have done something. Her loyalty to Cecelia made her think that she should go to the police about what her brother had done, but Cecelia said that she didn't want to press charges, so Hillary agreed to respect her wishes, but she still felt wrong about it.

"Whatever Brock is doing he gets himself into his own messes," Hillary said looking away from her mother.

"Do you know something about what Brock is up to? Every time I mention his name you give me this look like you are disgusted or horrified. If you know where your brother is you have to tell us Hillary."

"Brock has died to me a long time ago mom, and I assure you I have no idea where he is, but if I did I wouldn't have any problem telling you. The fact is he didn't tell me anything about where he was going or where he might be now. He hasn't told me anything in a long time. In fact he has hardly talked to me in a long time other than to argue with me or to say how I was brainwashed."

"But I just hate what the political situation has done to this country, it's ripping apart families and it's ripping apart the entire country."

Hillary shook her head. "It's not me was ripping apart the country, it's people like Brock, they refused to accept the results of the election no matter how many courts have said that the results are legitimate. People like Brock want a dictatorship."

Jessica shook her head. "Just please don't bring up any of these topics when your grandfather and grandmother arrive for Thanksgiving dinner. I want to have a cordial and pleasant Thanksgiving. I know that a lot of people across the country right now are probably having some of the tensest thanksgivings ever, but I don't want us to be one of them."

"Hey I won't bring it up if grandpa doesn't bring it up, but you know that grandpa isn't one to keep his mouth shut on these issues."

That was when Hillary heard the doorbell rang and she was pleased to see that it was Jordan and not her grandfather. Although she had to admit that she had her misgivings because she knew that her grandfather was a terrible bigot and didn't know that she was dating a black guy, and she was really worried about what might happen, but she had already prepped Jordan about the fact that her grandfather was a little bit stuck in the past.

"Jordan I am so glad to see you, how are you doing," Hillary said as she hugged and kissed Jordan.

"They arrested my brother at a BlackLivesMatter protest," Jordan said. "He was there to protest the latest police killings. I still can't believe that those police officers got away with opening machine gun fire on an entire crowd of black protesters, and you know who took the side of the police officers of course. I am just glad that my brother didn't get hurt, but it's terrible that he is spending Thanksgiving in prison."

"I think that Donald Trump has become even more unhinged knowing that his days are numbered," Hillary said shaking her head. "Sometimes I honestly wonder and worry if he is just going to start a nuclear war or something just to keep himself in power. Who knows what he will do now that he knows that the end is approaching? At this point he figures he has nothing to lose and that makes him more dangerous than ever. Gassing protesters, mass arrests, entire cities on lockdown just because they oppose the president, while meanwhile he lets the people in support of him run wild through the streets."

Jordan nodded.

"Let's try not to mention any of that when my grandfather gets here because he is a little bit behind the times," Hillary said shaking her head and rolling her eyes. "And by behind the times I mean that he didn't realize that the 1950s are over."

Hillary and Jordan tried to relax and tried not to bring up any of the contentious things that were on their minds, whether it be the political situation or the situation with Cecelia. Jordan said that if he did see Brock he would like to kick Brock's ass himself, except for the fact he didn't want to end up in prison like his brother.

Eventually grandpa Edwin and grandma Ethel showed up at the door with grandpa wearing a Trump 2020 shirt and a MAGA hat but no sign of any type of mask.

"Grandma, grandpa, so nice to see you," Hillary said.

"I hope you are happy that your guy is bringing about the end of America," Edwin said.

"Now dad we want to try to be cordial to one another and avoid any type of contentious discussion this Thanksgiving," Paul said. "This should be about togetherness, not division."

Edwin shook his head. "I'm sorry but I'm just a little bit disturbed that our democracy has been stolen from us and that our country is about to be taken over by some type of radical socialist who is going to descend our country into anarchy. And you'll notice that he is always hiding, hiding in his basement, I call him hidin' Biden."

"Grandfather I think that when tons of people are threatening your life on a daily basis you might want to keep a low profile," Hillary said trying to bite her tongue.

"Okay you two I think that there has been enough of that," Jessica said.

"Well let's sit down and have our last Thanksgiving dinner together before the country is ripped apart by anarchy and civil war," Edwin said as they sat down at the table. "Do you mind if I say grace or would that offend the unbeliever?"

Hillary's grandfather had never quite accepted the fact that she was an atheist and said that he prayed for her soul every day. To say that they didn't see eye to eye on spiritual matters or political matters was an understatement.

"Contrary to popular belief not every atheist is out to oppress you grandfather," Hillary said.

"Dear Jesus we thank you for this food that we are about to receive and we pray for your guidance in the troubled times that we have ahead," Edwin said as he began coughing very loudly.

"Dad you should really be wearing a mask," Paul said.

"I don't need no stupid masks," Edwin said as he continued coughing. "I'm no namby-pamby who feels that I need some type of mask to protect me. I'm not some type of germophobic person who thinks that this virus is coming to get me. The whole thing is totally inflated and it isn't really as bad as people think it is."

"Dad you live in Florida where there has been a new outbreak this fall, you really should be wearing a mask," Paul said. "We have seen the virus coming back with a resurgence, and it's just not really responsible of you to be risking your health like that. We are just worried about you."

"Well you shouldn't be, worry about your children," Edwin said. "Have you heard from Brock?"

Jessica shook her head. "Unfortunately we have not heard from Brock but we are praying every day for his safe return."

"That Brock is a good kid, I always thought that he would end up being a police officer like me someday," Edwin said. "Of course I don't envy modern-day cops who can't even do their job without 1 million protesters losing their shit every time they kill a person in the line of duty. Every time a police officer kills a black man no matter how guilty he is you have 1 million of these BlackLivesMatter protesters and anarchists wanting to defund the police so that they can riot and bring this country further into anarchy. We should lock all of them up. I guess we should just be glad now that we still have Donald Trump as our president for another couple of weeks at least, and maybe he can try to restore some order before Biden takes over and completely destroys the country and lets it self-destruct under his watch."

"Dad we agreed that we weren't going to make things contentious here," Paul said as he looked over at Jordan who looked decidedly very uncomfortable and clearly was trying hard to hold his tongue so as not to make a bad situation worse.

"Oh I see," Edwin said as he looked over at Jordan was sort of a dismissive look that said, I guess we can't talk about this with one of them here.

Grandma Ethel simply sat there saying little and just sort of smiling politely. Hillary had to admit that she always thought it was terrible the grandma Ethel was pretty much never saying anything. They often called her silent Ethel because they knew the grandpa had a belief that women were meant to be seen and not heard. She also knew that Edwin was very firmly pro-life and was elated when Ruth Bader Ginsburg died and was hoping that they would finally outlaw abortion, and practically had a heart attack when someone suggested the possibility that the court would be stacked to give it a liberal majority once again.

"So who wants to eat some turkey," Jessica said smiling as

Ethel simply smiled and nodded back, again not saying anything.

Once they started eating things got better because with people's mouths full of food they weren't talking about any other contentious issues. But everybody kept looking up every time Edwin started coughing.

"Dad are you sure that you are okay, maybe you should go see a doctor," Paul said.

"Doctors, what the hell do they know," Edwin said before grabbing his throat and coughing even more loudly than before.

For a moment it looked like grandma Ethel was about to say something as everyone could clearly see from the look on her face that she was worried, but she wasn't one to challenge her husband or to give him advice, so everyone just kept ignoring him as he continued coughing until it got so bad that it looked like he was having trouble breathing.

"Dad are you okay?" Paul asked again, as he could see that things were clearly not all right.

"I think that maybe we had better call an ambulance," Jessica said as she stood up.

"Oh dear," grandma Ethel said in barely a whisper before she covered up her mouth as though by speaking she had committed some type of cardinal sin against God before making the sign of the cross. It was the first thing that she had said all night.

As an ambulance came and took away grandfather Edwin grandma Ethel joined him and that was pretty much the end of their Thanksgiving dinner.

"Thank you for a lovely Thanksgiving dinner but I think I had be better getting home to my family because we still want to go visit my brother in prison," Jordan said.

Hillary hugged and kissed Jordan very tightly and looked him right in the eye. "Thank you from the bottom of my heart as I don't deserve a boyfriend like you. I am so sorry how awkward this was, and I think that you were a saint for not making a big deal of it."

Jordan laughed. "Believe it or not I have had more awkward Thanksgiving dinners before, so it's no big deal. I just hope your grandfather is okay."

"Don't worry he's a trooper, I'm sure he will be fine," Hillary said. But as Jordan left and Hillary sat down on the couch with her parents and considered the fact that the country was in a state of chaos, her grandfather was probably infected with coronavirus because of his own carelessness, and she still didn't know where her brother was or what he was up to, she was never more certain that things weren't going to be fine, not at all.

6

Grandpa Edwin was taken to the hospital quickly where he was diagnosed with the coronavirus. He insisted until the end that the coronavirus was most likely a hoax and he refused to wear a mask in the hospital, shouting and yelling at the nurses the whole time. Within a short order he found himself on a ventilator fighting for his life and after just one week his life was over.

Hillary had to admit she felt bad that their last exchange was sort of a hostile one, but she realized that her grandfather was probably too old to change. She kept telling herself that he was just from another era and that she couldn't change everybody or make everybody see the light, but she always felt like a personal failure, like she was walking away from trying to challenge people's prejudices, and she still felt bad about the way her grandfather had treated Jordan, and she knew that Jordan felt really bad about the whole situation as well, even though he was too polite to say anything about that.

Hillary and her entire family, as well as Jordan, all had to self-isolate for several weeks as they were worried that they had been infected with the coronavirus by grandpa Edwin. Fortunately it turned out not to be the case probably because they only had a limited amount of contact with him.

Because of the self-isolation however there was no funeral for grandpa Edwin as the coronavirus cases continued to surge. In fact the month of December saw some of the highest death tolls from the coronavirus as people continue to ignore social distancing guidelines and as Donald Trump continued to incompetently oversee the crisis, denying also the many who suffered adverse reactions to his miracle October surprise of a vaccine. She felt the fact that he knew he was going to be out of power soon meant that he simply didn't care at that point, not that he ever cared, as he only cared about how the virus made him look, not that it was killing people.

As the month of December slugged on Donald Trump became more and more erratic, tweeting dozens of times a day about how Biden was going to end up destroying the country, and that only by overturning the results of the election and keeping him in power could America be saved from its own self-destruction.

For their part Donald Trump supporters continued marching in the streets, mostly without masks and even in the dead cold of winter. Hillary didn't want to call what was going on a Civil War but more and more people were saying the word civil war every day.

She wasn't exactly sure what qualified as an actual civil war, in fact that was a matter of debate throughout the entire country. Was a bunch of people rioting in the streets considered to be a Civil War? She figured it had to be something more than that, but whatever was going on in the country it didn't bode well for the future. Even if we were going to get a more competent president who believed in science, between the social disorder and the division from the results of the election, as well as the continuing raging out of control of the coronavirus it did look like the country was going to hell in a hand basket, and Hillary sometimes wondered if our country could even last another month until Biden took office. It seemed like Trump was entirely hell-bent on taking the entire country down with him. If he couldn't be in charge he figured that no one should be.

Hillary didn't like to make the Hitler comparison but she had to admit Donald Trump seemed to have the same policy towards the American people that Hitler did towards the German people towards the end. In the end if they weren't going to continue to support him they could just as well die, and that pretty much summed things up.

One day while Hillary was in the mall looking for a Christmas present for Jordan something happened. She had just picked out the perfect facemask that said BlackLivesMatter on it. She knew that Jordan would get a kick out of that, although she wasn't sure if it was an appropriate gift to get given that his brother was still in prison.

Hillary had to admit that she was feeling more worried about

Jordan as time went on. She knew that he was always a peaceful person, but as the possibility of an actual civil war loomed she knew that he was beginning to prepare for the worst. As police shootings continued out of control and BlackLivesMatter protesters continued to clash with Trump supporters, many cities started to come under the control of martial law, or something very close to it at any rate. Again it was all the cities that opposed Donald Trump rather than the ones that supported him, in cities that supported him his supporters were able to go wild destroying property, with Donald Trump and his supporters being completely hypocritical to the end.

Jordan wanted to raise some bail to get his brother out of prison but they simply could not get the money. And then Donald Trump passed an executive order that people who were arrested during protests and violent acts of anarchy should be treated as enemy combatants and not entitled to the same rights as they had been before, which made a whole situation that was bad even more complicated and worse.

After Hillary had finished paying for the facemask she was walking through the mall, which she had to admit was not as crowded as it had been in previous years, thanks to the epidemic. In fact Trump even went on TV saying that this would probably be the last year we could say Merry Christmas. It was amazing how full of shit he was and what a persecution complex that he and his followers had. They were the real snowflakes as far as she was concerned. She didn't have an aneurysm when somebody wished her a Merry Christmas, but whenever she said happy holidays to someone she got some disapproving stares as though she had mortally offended them.

She decided she would go to the food court to get something to eat and that was when she saw him. It was Brock, she was sure of it. She wasn't exactly sure what she should do. This was the first that she had seen of him since he had run away from home, the same day that Cecelia had accused him of the most horrible thing that he had ever done in a long list of terrible things he had done over the course of his life.

At first she decided that she was going to approach him but as she started walking towards him she found herself hesitating. What exactly what she going to say to him? Was she just going to go up and say hi, by the way I heard you raped my friend?

She began walking away when all of a sudden she felt a hand on her shoulder and turned around and staring at her was Brock, wearing a mask simply because they wouldn't let anyone in the mall without one, so she couldn't exactly see the look on his face, as to whether he was smiling or frowning or scowling.

"Brock," was all she could say.

"Hillary," he said, and the two of them stood there with a long awkward pause.

"So where the hell have you been?" Hillary finally managed to ask.

"That's none of your business," Brock said shaking his head. "Let's just say I am with a good group of people who are trying to preserve our way of life in this country, a group of true patriots still loyal to the true leader of this country, not the usurper."

Hillary wanted to say that a usurper was one who tried to take power from legitimately elected individual, but she knew it was pointless to argue with him. As far as he was concerned, and as far as millions of Americans were concerned, it didn't matter what the election said, as far as they were concerned their country had been stolen from them by an illegitimate election.

Hillary wanted to say something about Cecelia but she wasn't sure if she should say that in the middle of a mall like that. On the other hand she was thinking that Brock probably wouldn't try anything in a public place like that, and that she could always run away and scream if he tried anything.

"Mom and dad are worried about you," she finally said, not sure exactly what else to say to him at the moment.

"Well they shouldn't be, I'm doing fine. They should be worried about the state of this country."

"You know not everything is about politics Brock. Did you know that grandpa Edwin died? He died of the coronavirus that you keep saying is a hoax and that seems to be killing thousands of people every day. But I guess that's all just a bunch of fake news and lies created by the liberal media, right?"

"Look I know you don't believe in authority and Law and Order and that you want to devote your life to defending criminals –

" Brock began to say before she began shaking her head.

"Says the juvenile delinquent," Hillary said all of the sudden remembering Cecelia and wanting to smack Brock hard across his face.

"Look just tell mom and dad that I am okay if you want to tell them that you saw me at all."

"I guess I can't count on telling them that you're going to be home for Christmas, can I?"

Brock stood there staring at her and she couldn't tell the expression on his face because he was wearing a mask, so she was having a hard time reading his emotions or his sincerity. She was about to say something else when all of a sudden Brock just shook his head and started walking away.

She felt like she should follow him and go after him. She felt that she should have confronted him about what he had done to Cecelia. She felt like she should have said something or done something, anything, but as she watched Brock walking away she realized that there was no point in saying anything further to him. He was basically a lost cause and as far as she knew and for all that she cared she would never see him again, this being one last chance meeting. But at the end of the day even if that was the case she didn't really have anything else to say to him, and she didn't figure that she had anything to say to her parents about him either. So in the end when she got home she never mentioned that she saw Brock at the mall, and she figured that that was for the best, as she didn't want to get her parents' hopes up for nothing.

December 25, 2020, Christmas day.

It was a quiet and somber Christmas that year. Between the political situation, the coronavirus and the death of grandpa Edwin everybody was feeling less than cheerful and in the holiday spirit.

Hillary looked at her parents and she could see that as they hung up a stocking for Brock that it was killing them. Hillary didn't even know why they were bothering doing it as she felt like it was the ultimate in false hope. Put up a stocking and maybe Brock would somehow come home. As an atheist she didn't believe in such a superstition like that, but as a human being she couldn't deny her parents anything that would make them feel better, however irrational or illogical it was.

She had seen Jordan early that morning and given him his gift, and as far as she could tell he looked like he liked it. He got her a proud to be a liberal shirt that she thought looked pretty good on her, but she had to admit that it was a little bit tight and it sort of accentuated her cleavage, and she couldn't help but wonder if maybe that was why Jordan picked it out. He was woke, but he was still a guy. But either way she felt that it was a thoughtful gift and she liked it. Jordan was going to be spending Christmas visiting his brother in prison. She could only hope that once Biden came to power that some of these people, who had been arrested for spurious reasons, most likely for nothing more than the color of their skin, would finally have their day in court with legal rights restored.

With less than a month to go until the inauguration she was just hoping that the country could hold on until then and that once Biden came into office that things would just suddenly work out. But she knew better than to naïvely believe that everything was going to be okay just because Biden won the election. There was still uncertainty as to whether Trump would willingly leave office, and if he didn't leave office it would precipitate a constitutional crisis never before seen in the country, and she could only hope that the rule of law would prevail. But already the military was discussing what they would do in such a situation like that, and just the fact that it was a matter of debate was enough to make anyone nervous.

"Well now that everybody is here why don't we sit down for our Christmas dinner," Jessica said.

They all felt sad as they looked at the seat where normally grandpa Edwin would be sitting. Hillary had to admit that even though they never saw eye to eye on anything she still missed her grandfather and thought that it was a shame he died simply because he wouldn't wear a mask. He was stubborn until the end, and she would almost admire him for that, if it weren't for the fact that he was stubborn about all the wrong things.

They all sat down and began eating but they didn't eat for very long when all of a sudden they heard a knock at the door.

"I'll get it," Hillary said kind of wondering who it would be and was surprised when she opened the door and standing there was Brock.

"Who is it dear," Jessica said as she went over and saw Brock standing there causing her to drop her glass on the floor. "Brock! Oh my darling baby boy where have you been?" Jessica ran over and hugged Brock who simply gave her an indifferent stare.

Brock let himself into the house and walked over to the table where Paul looked at him and shook his head. "So the prodigal son returns. Where the hell have you been?"

"I'm not here to stay," Brock said shaking his head. "I just wanted to pick up a couple of things."

"And you chose Christmas as just a random day to do that?" Paul asked.

"I also wanted to say Merry Christmas, you know while it is still legal," Brock said as he looked at Hillary with an angry glare.

"Well Merry Christmas brother," Hillary said. "Happy holidays as well."

Hillary wasn't exactly sure what else to say to her brother and thought that he had a lot of nerve showing up like that only to leave right away.

"Do you have any idea how worried we have been about you?" Jessica said. "We were worried that you were hurt or that you were killed in all of the violence going on in the country. After you disappeared we called all of the prisons to make sure that you weren't under arrest or something. Do you have any idea how much stress you have been causing your father and I?"

Brock smirked. "Don't worry mom, far from it, in fact I am staying with a bunch of true patriots who are going to restore law and order to this unruly country and restore the legitimate leader of this country to power, before it self-destructs from the inside out and is taken over by the Chinese and the Mexicans."

"Son it's over," Paul said shaking his head. "Look I supported Trump and everything but it's over, he lost the election and we just have to accept that. It's not going to be the end of the world or the end of America."

Brock shook his head. "How wrong and naïve you are. Look I am not here to convert any of you and I wouldn't expect you to understand. I just came to get my things and then I will be on my way."

Brock walked into his room and started gathering up a bag of a couple of his more prized possessions, not that he had anything that Hillary thought was of much value, like lots of old trophies and stuff.

"Say something dear," Jessica said as she elbowed Paul but he simply shook his head.

"Brock is a man, he is legally an adult and if he doesn't want to stay here then he doesn't have to," Paul said. "You know Brock you are always welcome to stay here but we want to know what you are up to and want to know that you are okay."

"Don't worry dad I'm not going to be your problem anymore," Brock said as he finished packing his things. "In fact I was just about ready to start leaving."

"Brock please, it's Christmas, why don't you spend Christmas with your family," Jessica said. "Are you hungry? I know that you love my turkey, and since you missed it on Thanksgiving I figure why you don't just stay and have dinner with us? Whatever is going on in your life, whatever is bothering you, we can talk about it, we are your family and you can always come to us when you are having a problem."

Brock shook his head. "The problem I have isn't something that can be solved through a family dinner mom. The problem I have goes right down to the root issues destroying this country. I'm going to be part of something bigger than myself and I think that you're going to be proud of me. But I have to do this on my own, so I am sorry but I will be leaving."

Jessica started running after Brock but as he slammed the door behind him causing the Christmas wreath to fall off on the floor Jessica, Paul and Hillary could just stand there looking at each other not saying anything and not sure what to say or do next.

"That boy ain't right, now come sit down and eat," grandma Ethel said.

As the three of them turned to grandma Ethel, who had spoken for the first time all night, they figured that the least they could do in response to something as dramatic as her actually speaking was to listen to her. So the three of them took one last look at the door, put the wreath back up and then the three of them sat down with grandma Ethel and had Christmas dinner together as a family, but without Brock.

7

Monday, January 11, 2021.

Much like the previous attack that also took place on the 11th, every single American knew where they were when they first heard the news. Hillary was in her government class during her first couple of days at college when she heard the news.

"And as we have seen through studying history it is easy to see how in times of crisis even liberal democratic societies find their democratic norms being challenged," the professor said as he wrote democratic norms challenged on the blackboard. "This is an appropriate lesson to keep in mind today as we prepare for the transition of power from one president to another. The peaceful transition of power is vital to any democracy, and that is why for your assignments for the end of the month I want you to write up a report on the transition of power from Donald Trump to Joe Biden and what it says about democratic norms in America."

Fate has a way of being strange and synchronistic in many cases and this was one of those days. That was when a woman came into the class and waved Professor Ryan out of the classroom to tell him something. All of the students in the class began murmuring to themselves before professor Ryan came back into the class.

"Students it is my terrible duty to inform you that classes have been canceled for the rest of the day," Prof. Ryan said. "I have just been informed that there was a massive terrorist attack on Trump Tower in New York City that is believed to have killed upwards of 1000 Americans. Therefore class is now dismissed and may God help us all."

Hillary didn't exactly believe that God was going to help, and she wished at that moment that she was one of those people who honestly believed that there was a just higher power that was looking out for the world. But it was things like this more than anything else that caused her to doubt that was the case.

"What do you think this means for the peaceful transition of power," Hillary's classmate Rhonda said as they walked out of the classroom into the hallways, which were filled with students looking panicked, but with a couple with smiles on their face.

"It looks like someone finally gave Trump what he deserved," someone said in the hallway. "I hope he was in the tower at the time."

Hillary and Rhonda immediately went to the nearest television where Donald Trump was giving a press conference on the terrorist attack.

"This is an outrageous and cowardly terrorist attack both on the nation of America and against me personally," Donald Trump said. "I am glad to tell the American people however that I am okay and that my family is okay and that none of us were in the tower at the time."

"Yeah because that's what we care about the most, we care about you being alive," Hillary said rolling her eyes as Rhonda shook her head. "It's amazing that even in a moment of crisis where over 1000 people have died Donald Trump's first priority still remains and ever will be Donald Trump."

"But we will not allow our country to descend into even further anarchy," Donald Trump said with a look both of terror but also something of an evil smirk. Hillary could swear that he seemed like he was smirking over something. "That is why I am going to ask Congress to declare sweeping executive powers so that I can deal with this crisis without delay. Our country is under terrorist attack and we are on full alert. We don't know who has perpetrated this cowardly attack but you had better believe me that I take this very personally. That is why I am calling for an order of martial law in New York City effective this evening. Anyone caught out after curfew walking the streets will be immediately arrested as an enemy combatant."

"I can't believe it, the fucker is actually going to do it," Rhonda said. "This is his bid to make himself dictator with less than 10 days left before his presidency is supposed to finally come to an inglorious end."

Hillary suddenly felt sick to her stomach as she shook her

head. "Normally I am the last person to give into the idea of conspiracy theories but I think that this is just too perfect as far as the timing goes. I agree with you, fully, this is his last bid to remain in power by any means necessary. A national crisis due to terrorism is just what he needs to suspend the Constitution and to keep him in power."

"He said that he wasn't going to allow a peaceful transference of power if he lost the election and I think now we are seeing just how dangerous things are," Rhonda said. "I need to call my family, I have family in New York and they are probably freaking out about this."

That was when Hillary suddenly remembered that Samantha was in New York, as she was going to college in New York City. She immediately got out her phone and started dialing in a panic.

"Before you say anything else I want to let you know that I am completely fine physically," Samantha said. "But I think that you know that I am freaking out as much as I am sure that you are freaking out over this. I can actually see the remains of the tower smoldering from my window."

"I think you should do everything in your power to try and get out of the city right now," Hillary said. "I don't know what's going to happen, but I know that whatever it is it's going to be bad, like after Pearl Harbor level bad. This isn't just a repeat of 9/11, this is something else altogether."

"I don't want to say the words but I know that you are thinking them as well."

"False flag."

"I never believed that there was a conspiracy on 9/11 but I think that this is still comparable to the Reichstag fire. Donald Trump knows that the only way he is going to stay in power now is if he completely revokes the Constitution and continues maintaining power by force."

"Samantha, like I said, I think that you should get out of there right now."

"Believe me that was my first thought as well but they are closing off all exits to the city. They are shutting down the subways, and we already have soldiers marching through the streets. They are arresting anyone in the vicinity of the tower, anyone who looks suspicious, and by suspicious I mean nonwhite."

"I think that I had better call Jordan, I want you to say strong Samantha and stay vigilant and keep your eyes peeled. Right now we don't know who we can trust but I know that we certainly can't trust the people in power."

Hillary immediately began dialing Jordan who called her before she could finish dialing.

"Jordan I was just now calling you, I guess we really are psychically in tuned," Hillary said.

Jordan laughed. "I know it's not funny but I know if you are accepting the possible existence of psychic power than you really are as nervous as I am. But before you ask I am okay, how are you doing?"

"As well as anyone can expect to be when a misogynistic racist egomaniac is setting up a dictatorship to keep him in power. Jordan I think that for your best safety and everything – "

"I know you don't have to tell me twice, stay off the streets and keep a low profile. Right now I just being a black man on the streets is probably enough to get me arrested, I mean more so than usual, the fact that my brother is a criminal means that I'm probably going to become under suspicion myself."

"Stay strong Jordan I promise I will call you every day while this crisis is going on. This is the time when we all have to come together and unite against the forces of evil. If America wasn't fascist before, if we weren't in a civil war before, I think we definitely are now."

Hillary and Jordan said their goodbyes and turned off the phone. Hillary immediately wanted to get on the Internet to learn as much about the attacks as possible but when she went to check social media she found out the twitter was locked down and that nobody could post anything. If twitter was being shut down over this she knew it was something big.

"Shutting down social media, one of the best ways to silence all opposition," Hillary said shaking her head. "The only good thing at least is that he won't be able to tweet either. I suppose the possibility of losing power is the only thing that would actually cause him to go as far as to shut down his main source of communication with the American people."

Hillary was trying to calm down but it seemed like things were moving fast. She felt like probably all major forms of communication were being watched right now and shut down. She thought that maybe it was for the best because she didn't want to say anything that was going to get her swept up and rounded up into a concentration camp.

She decided to try and turn to the regular media, who were all reporting on the crisis, and she could see that most people are freaking out just as much as she was. Then as she was watching a newscaster accused Donald Trump of trying to use the crisis to install himself as dictator suddenly the channel was shut down altogether.

That was when Hillary remembered something she had read a long time ago. She knew that in times of major crisis the government theoretically had the power to take control of all forms of communication and to shut down all opposition and to seize control of all media. This is exactly what Donald Trump had wanted from the beginning, now he could legitimately start arresting journalists simply for doing their job.

As she watched the TV she saw Vladimir Putin coming on giving his heartfelt condolences to the people of America and to his good friend Donald Trump. Was Putin in on all of this? Was this actually some way of Russia trying to finally take over after they failed to stop Donald Trump from taking control through 'legitimate' electoral means?

Hillary spent the rest of the day making phone calls and trying to find any information she could about what was going on as more and more forms of media was shut down. There was a full media blackout but word quickly got around that mass arrests were going on and that they were sending soldiers to television stations and to newspapers to occupy them. All protesters were being arrested and many were being gassed and tasered and some even shot.

Finally after an exhausting day Hillary got to sleep somehow but she knew that her sleep would be troubled and that it would most likely be full of all sorts of nightmares that she couldn't even begin to imagine would now be intruding on reality.

8

January 12, 2021.

"It is not possible to facilitate a peaceful transition of power when the nation is under attack like this," Donald Trump said as he gave a press conference. "I encourage all Americans to obey the law as we will continue to have law, we will continue to have order, I will not let this nation slip into chaos under my watch and I am still the legitimate president of the United States."

Members of the press began asking Donald Trump about Biden taking power.

"Trying to transition from one president to another while the country is actively under attack and where I am actively under attack would be reckless and irresponsible," Donald Trump said. "The inauguration of Joe Biden won't be happening until this crisis is over."

Reports came on the television of Joe Biden being taken into protective custody for his own safety as it was believed that this was a coordinated attack not just against Donald Trump but the entire United States government. It didn't take the Republicans long to declare Donald Trump sweeping executive powers under the crisis that effectively suspended the Constitution and allowed military soldiers to occupy most major American cities.

"Jordan are you there?" Hillary said as she frantically tried to reach him once again but received no answer from him until later that evening. "Jordan I finally reached you, where have you been?"

"I was taken in for questioning by a bunch of guys with guns who wanted to ask if I was part of the terrorist organization known as BlackLivesMatter and whether I collaborated with my brother, who I can't seem to reach under the current circumstances, who is imprisoned as an enemy combatant."

"Oh my God Jordan, I'm so sorry, but you're okay right?"

"I'm not in prison right now, so I guess I am doing okay on that level, but I am most certainly not all right. I think you know as well as I do that this is Donald Trump trying to cement his power as dictator. At this point he has absolutely nothing to lose so he is putting all the cards on the table and trying to maneuver himself into power as dictator. I think he knows that if he doesn't do this he is going to be removed from power and probably face all sorts of criminal investigations. This is the end game Hillary, this is going to determine whether America is going to be a democracy anymore or whether we are just going to be one more dictatorship."

"I wish I could say I disagree with you but I think that most people can see the writing on the wall. But the sad thing is that Donald Trump and his supporters have already basically granted him the power of a dictator. I don't know what legal means we now have to stop him from continuing to hold onto power."

"You know that I am nonviolent but a quote comes to mind, those who make peaceful revolution impossible make violent revolution inevitable."

"Jordan what exactly are you saying?"

"What I'm saying that if it comes down to it I am willing to fight to stop this. I am willing to take up arms against the United States government and restore it to its legitimate democratically elected leader. The time for debate is no longer here, this is the time for action. Donald Trump is not playing by the rules anymore, not that he ever was, but now he has thrown the rulebook right out the window and into a burning fire pit that could consume us all. If he is not going to play by the rules everything is on the table, including armed revolution. I'm not the only one who thinks this Hillary; I can tell you that a large majority of my friends and family think that this is going to be the beginning of the next American Civil War."

"Don't do anything that you're going to regret Jordan or do anything rash, we just have to think this through."

"I think you know that I have thought this through in detail and you know where I stand on this. There's going to be a march on Washington and I am going to be there when it happens. I'm not asking you to come with me, as no one can make that decision but you, but I know that when it comes down to it I'm going to march and fight for my freedom like Martin Luther King, like Malcolm X, and like my brother. But I don't know if it is safe to talk on this line as who knows whether the government is bugging me? I may be very well on my way to a concentration camp now. But don't worry I will keep in touch with you and I will continue to call you every couple of hours to let you know that I am safe. But I want you to stay safe yourself Hillary. You know that I love you and that I will always love you, and I don't think that I could live with myself if anything happens to you."

"I love you too Jordan, stay safe," she said as they ended the call. She immediately began dialing Samantha.

"Oh Hillary they are marching in the streets, people are clashing with the police and the military and they have opened fire on protesters in the crowd. People are resisting the mass arrests, people are calling it a revolution but hundreds are being shot and being killed. They aren't showing this on television, the full media blackout is trying to suppress the truth of what is going on, but the people cannot deny it anymore."

"Jordan said that he's going to go down to Washington, says he's going to take up arms. This is getting out of control Samantha."

"Oh it's been out of control for a very long time, now the shit has hit the fan and everybody has to take a stand, whether they are for liberal democracy or whether they are for a fascist dictatorship. At this point Donald Trump isn't even trying to hide it anymore and he is rallying his supporters to come to his aid."

"I hate to say it but –"

"I know you don't want to think about Brock right now, and I know you haven't wanted to think about him for the last several months, but I think that we both know where he stands and who he is with right now. I have no doubt that he is most likely in Washington and probably is heavily armed. You know that he worships the ground that Donald Trump walks on and believes that he is the second coming of Jesus in the flesh. I have no doubt that he would willingly die for Donald Trump and probably is planning to. I can't imagine what your family must be going through right now."

"You know after what he did on Christmas I figured I had pretty much written him out of my life, but in spite of everything deep in the pit of my heart I feel a stirring of sorrow, and God help me, in spite of everything, in spite of the fact that I don't believe in God, I am still willing to swear to God that I don't want my brother to die. As much as I have come to hate him over these last couple of years and months I don't want him to throw his life away defending a tyrant like Donald Trump. I like to believe that in his heart of hearts he could still see the light and gain some type of redemption, but I just don't know if he can. If this is going to be a Civil War I know we are going to be on opposite sides and I know there is no reasoning with him."

"You know Hillary I support you in whatever you do. In fact if New York City wasn't under martial law I would try to leave and go to Washington myself. But this is a time when you have to do what you have to do and everyone has to make that decision for themselves. But please be safe and continue to call me and let me know that you are okay each day. Do you understand Hillary?"

"Yes, I fully understand and I will talk to you soon," Hillary said as she put down her phone. As she stared out at the coverage on the news of cities going up in smoke and people clashing with the police and the military she understood one thing, she knew very firmly where she stood and who she stood with.

She knew that she was going to Washington.

9

January 15, 2021, Washington DC.

"I am glad to see that there are still patriots who care about seeing that this country is not going to descend into total anarchy or into socialism," Donald Trump said on television from the Oval Office. "Your nation has called to you and you have answered that call and you are not going to allow a usurper to use their illegitimate election to take power from the rightful leader of this country. That is why I am now calling for the arrest of Joe Biden until it can be determined that he had nothing to do with the terrorist attack on Trump Tower."

As Brock lined up on the streets leading to the White House with his assault rifle in his hands he had to admit he was feeling really good, proud to be defending Donald Trump from those who would remove him from office and preserving his way of life. As he stood there with many other proud boys he knew that this was going to be a day that would live down in world history and he was glad that he would be part of it.

"We are finally going to get to shoot some liberals," said Bruce, one of his fellow soldiers in Donald Trump's ragtag army. "They were stupid to pick a fight with us. They are the people who want gun-control but it's the people with the guns who will always determine the course of history. We are going to save this country from the liberals and the socialists and the atheists and the homosexuals and the feminists and the Mexicans and the Blacks and the Jews and the pedophiles at the pizza place. There are just so many degenerates in this country that I can't even list them all, it really is sickening isn't it?"

Brock nodded in agreement but in the pit of his stomach she felt some type of fear. "Do you think that the military is going to side with us and the legitimate president or do you think that they are going to defect to Biden and try to carry out the coup against our great leader?"

"Not if we have anything to say about it," Bruce said as he started stroking his gun in a masturbatory way. As part of the proud boys creed that they'd agreed not to masturbate but as far as Bruce was concerned this didn't exactly count, but for the time being it was a decent enough substitute for the sin of self-pleasuring.

"I am just worried. If the military sides with Biden I don't know if we have enough forces to fight them off. I mean we are just sort of a militia, that's the actual United States military. I don't actually have any military training, and while I talk a big game I've never shot at other people before in actual armed combat."

Bruce shook his head. "I am sure that once the military starts marching on the city and they realize that the American people want Donald Trump to remain in power they will join with us. They are not going to shoot the American people who are defending the legitimate president of the United States, who God willing will be our president until the day he dies, by which time hopefully he will complete his God given role to make this country great again before the liberals, illegals, feminists, secularists, queers and niggers ruined it."

"We can only pray to our Christian God that that is the case. But I do believe that God is with us and that God will bring about victory for his representative on earth, Donald Trump."

"Thank God for Donald Trump and God bless him and God bless America." Bruce made the sign of the cross and stroked his gun some more.

Donald Trump paced around the Oval Office feeling more nervous by the moment.

"I am pleased to see that there are many patriots out there today," Donald Trump said as he looked at all the members of the proud boys and other militias who had come to his defense.

"Word is that the majority of the military is siding with Biden," said one of Donald Trump's military advisers. "Maybe we should flee. I don't know if these people are well-trained enough to stand up to the United States military. They don't believe that you are legitimate, although there is major division in the ranks. There are many who believe that you are illegitimate but there is a sizable portion who believes that the election really was rigged."

"Of course it was rigged, there's no way I could have lost otherwise," Donald Trump said as he gestured wildly with his hands. "Do you doubt that this election was stolen from me?"

"No, of course not Mr. President. You are of course the legitimate president of the United States and anyone who believes otherwise is just a traitor."

"Maybe we should pray," Mike Pence said.

Donald Trump tried to keep a straight face. He still couldn't believe that he had so many Christian supporters who actually believed that he was on their side. He felt quite pleased with himself so that he was able to manipulate so many ignorant people into supporting him. He couldn't believe that there were actually people who thought that he was Christlike. Even Mike Pence seemed to have bought into his bullshit.

Donald Trump smiled. "I think it's pretty clear that God is on our side, praise be to his name."

Mike Pence nodded his head and got down on his hands and knees and started to lead everyone in a prayer for victory.

"I had better make another announcement to my followers," Donald Trump said as he went on video. "Fellow patriots, today you are going to defend your nation's capital against the usurper and his military forces. Today you are going to determine whether the United States is going to remain the world's greatest nation, or whether the world's greatest democracy is going to be overthrown by the forces of fanatics who want to impose socialism, who want to take your guns, who want to demean your religion and rewrite history to erase your glorious heritage. But with faith in God I believe that we will succeed this day. The choice with you is today, defend me and defend the country, defend Law and Order, or see your country destroyed and ripped apart by anarchy, standby."

Brock smiled. "Inspiring words from the greatest speaker of our generation, now let's let the bloodbath begin!"
Everyone on the streets lining the White House raised their guns and started letting out a cheer. There were people waving their Trump banners and holding up their MAGA hats, others were waving Confederate flags and several waving swastikas as well.
"We've got the real true blooded Americans here," Bruce said. "Real pure salt of the earth people, the liberals don't have a chance against us."

"Jordan I have to admit that I am very afraid," Hillary said. "I have always been a social justice warrior but not like a literal warrior who fights in combat. I don't even know how to fire a gun."
Jordan put his arm on her shoulder. "Hillary if you are afraid I would understand if you went back, and I don't want anything to happen to you. This is not necessarily going to be a military confrontation. We are hoping that when millions of people march on Washington peacefully that the people defending Donald Trump will stand down. And once they see that we have the weight of the military on our side I think that they will surrender immediately. They know that they are no match for the United States military. For all their talk of the military glory and all of this patriotic stuff that they speak of, these are just a bunch of militias, they don't love this country, they just hate people of color. They want to return this country to a country of segregation, to a country for just the privileged, for just white men. The numbers alone are against them

and they are bound to fail."

"I just can't help but think of Brock. I know that he is one of the people who is in that crowd who might be firing on us. I always knew that it might come down to brother fighting brother and brother fighting sister, as it may be in this case, but the idea that my brother and I might be on opposite sides of a shooting match is just sickening to me. I don't even think that my parents have any idea that Brock is down there, but I know in my heart of hearts that must be where he is."

"Don't worry, it's going to be okay," Jordan said as he kissed her on the forehead as the train approached the city and the protesters got off.

"I guess it's now or never," Hillary said as she and Jordan started going out with the rest of the protesters. She could see that the streets were clogged for as far as the eye could see with people brandishing all sorts of signs demanding that Donald Trump step down from power peacefully.

"It looks like they are marching on us," Brock said as he could see the marchers coming towards them. "Supposedly they are peaceful but I can see that many of them are carrying weapons. Are we to open fire on them? I don't know how I feel about opening fire on a group of protesters. I mean they are insane and everything like that, but I've never actually killed someone before."

Bruce smiled. "Don't lose your resolve, we are the true Patriots, and sometimes the blood of patriots has to be spilled to renew the soil or, I can't remember the exact quote, but the point is sometimes you have to die for what you believe in. And sometimes you have to kill for what you believe in. If you really believe in Donald Trump as the legitimate president of the United States you have to be willing to fight for that. We have gone this far and we're not going to give up now."

Brock was starting to feel misgivings. He had talked a big game but now that he saw huge crowds of people marching in their direction the thought of opening fire on them was beginning to give him butterflies in his stomach. He was beginning to think that maybe he had made the wrong choice and that maybe he should get out of there while he still could. He always thought that he could fire on people if he needed to, but now he wasn't quite so sure if he had the stomach for it.

One of the protesters came to the head of the crowd holding a bullhorn. "Donald Trump we are asking you to see reason and to step down peacefully. We have millions of Americans here marching on the city peacefully to ask you to step down from power so that the legitimate president could take office. There is still the possibility of peaceful transition of power. If you want to remain in power by force you know that you are fighting a losing battle."

From the Oval Office Donald Trump was listening to the protester and shaking his head. He knew that if he stepped down from power he would be immediately arrested and that he had nothing to lose at this point. He started to contemplate the nuclear launch codes, would he really be able to use that as a bargaining chip?

"Mr. President we await your response," the woman said as she put down the bullhorn.

"I'm going to give them the orders to open fire," Donald Trump said.

"But sir that's the American people out there, are you really going to tell your followers to open fire on civilians like that?" his military advisor asked.

"There is only one way to maintain Law and Order, and that is through the use of force, every legitimate leader throughout history has realized this fact," Donald Trump said. "It's times like these that separate the good presidents from the bad, and the great ones from the legitimate ones. And I am one of the great presidents, in fact I am the greatest president in American history, greater than Lincoln even, and today we are going to see the rebirth of a new nation. Today is the birth of a nation and I fully intend to be the new founding father."

"But sir those are the American people, I tell you again. I don't know if I could condone such an action."

"You're either with me or against me, now what's it going to be," Donald Trump said.

Brock stood there nervously clutching his gun and looking

out into the crowd. That was when he saw it, somewhere in the crowd he saw Hillary standing there with Jordan. She was near the front of the crowd and if they opened fire she would almost assuredly be hit.

Something began staring in Brock that he hadn't felt in a long time. As he looked upon his sister out there in the crowd suddenly didn't see a coward anymore. He thought to himself that she doesn't believe there is anything beyond this life and yet she was willing to risk her life to march for her ideals maybe she wasn't some type of spineless coward after all. He didn't agree with her beliefs, but at that moment he wasn't sure if he could raise his gun against her knowing that she was in the crowd and likely to be hit if gunshots were fired.

"Here it comes, today is the day we make history," Bruce said with a look of bloodlust in his eyes.

Brock continued staring ahead at the crowd and as he looked at his sister he felt like he was about to be sick and felt himself lowering his gun.

"People of the United States of America," a voice said that came over a loudspeaker system. "My name is Luis Meriwether, a descendent of one of the famous team of explorers, who can trace my ancestry back many generations to before this country even achieved its independence. I am a senior military advisor to the president and I come from a long line of military families. Your leader Donald Trump wanted you to open fire upon the American people, to fire upon civilians, to kill peaceful protesters. He cares nothing for the Constitution, he cares nothing for your lives, and he cares only about power and himself. I realized that if he was not removed from power it would effectively be the end of the American Republic and perhaps even democracy throughout the civilized world. In every man and every woman's life there comes a time when they have to make a choice as to where they stand. Are they going to stand for liberty and freedom and equality, or are they going to stand for tyranny, oppression, corruption and lies? Today I have made my decision, and with several members of the Secret Service and the United States military stationed within the White House itself we have done the right thing and we have arrested Donald Trump for treason against the United States of America. It is over, the Republic is restored. So I'm asking all of you standing outside with your guns poised and pointed at the American people to show some sanity, to show some decency, and to stand down and peacefully remove yourselves from the city and allow the true military to restore order. God bless the United States of America."

A silence came over the crowd. Nobody had seen this coming. Senior military officials within the White House itself who had previously been loyal to Trump had decided to do the right thing.

"Don't listen to him, it's fake news," Bruce said as he raised his gun and fired upon the woman who had the bullhorn and started firing randomly into the crowd who started running in all directions screaming.

"No!" Brock said as he turned his gun and opened fire on Bruce as several other people began firing wildly into the crowd. The last thing he remembered before blacking out was the sound of screaming.

10

January 20, 2021.

Brock slowly opened his eyes trying to remember what had happened and wondered where he was. He slowly sat up and felt a sharp blinding pain in the back of his head. But as he looked to his side that was when he saw someone he had never expected to see.

"Hillary," Brock said as he rubbed his eyes.

"Brock you're awake!" Hillary said as she hugged him.

"What happened?"

Hillary shook her head. "I know you're not going to like to hear this, but the military arrested Donald Trump and most of the senior members of his administration. Immediately many members of the administration were willing to squeal on him, all easily betraying one another towards the end in hopes of getting immunity for themselves. They revealed one of the most widespread conspiracies in American history. Donald Trump was all the time working for the Russians who wanted to install him as a puppet dictatorship as a way of taking over the United States. When they couldn't get him to continue in power by legitimate means they realized that the only thing that they could do was orchestrate a terrorist attack to justify a suspension of the Constitution. It was a false flag attack, Donald Trump directed his followers to detonate explosives in his own building as a way of generating sympathy for him and getting people to rally to his cause. He knew the only way he could avoid criminal investigations was to hold onto power by any means necessary. But it's all out in the open now and there have been arrests throughout the country. The military restored order temporarily until there can be a peaceful transition of power."

Brock stared at her, not exactly sure what to say, but he could still feel his head throbbing.

"I'm guessing you don't believe me do you," Hillary said as she shook her head. "The last couple of days have been some of the most dramatic days in the history of this country and the world at large."

"What happened to me I mean?" Brock said.

"You got shot in the head and lapsed into a coma. You have been unconscious for several days now and no one was sure if you would ever come out of it. It was chaos. Somebody fired into the crowd and then everything just went crazy but then the military came in and most of Donald Trump's supporters stood down, but many hundreds of them confronted the military saying the Donald Trump's arrest was fake news, but there has been a coup, a coup that removed Donald Trump from power, and now he is facing criminal charges. Again I know that he is your hero and that you probably aren't going to believe it no matter what the evidence says, and I know millions of others aren't going to believe the evidence either, but it's the truth Brock, and the sooner you accept it the easier it will be. Brock I know we have had our differences –"

"I know," Brock said as he raised his hand to try and silence her. "I don't know what I believe anymore Hillary. I just know that while I was in that coma, well you know how people who have almost died say that they have seen their entire life flashing before their eyes?"

Hillary nodded. "Yes, I have heard of that."

"Well look I know you don't believe in God or anything like that, but when I was in that coma I saw my entire life flashed before my eyes and I didn't necessarily like the person that I saw. Again maybe it was just a hallucination, I know you don't believe in God, but I had something of like a spiritual revelation, if that makes sense."

Hillary put her hand on Brock's. "I don't know what you experienced, but whatever it is it was real enough to you, and I am willing to accept that."

"I still don't agree with you and a lot of your beliefs, but when I saw you in that crowd I knew that I could not open fire. I knew that I could not shoot innocent people. I have had a lot of hate inside of me Hillary, and there is still a lot of hate inside of me, but I realized in that moment that for all our differences I don't hate you, and I did not want you to come to harm, and that I couldn't live with myself if I were responsible for that. Do you think you can ever forgive me?"

Hillary thought to Cecelia and everything that had happened in the last couple of months. She once again felt anger boiling up inside of herself, but as she looked to her brother, with a pleading look in his eyes, she felt that for the first time ever he was being sincere and that he was no longer looking upon her with hate.

"It's not me that you need to be asking for forgiveness," Hillary said. "But I am glad that you are alive."

"I am ready to accept responsibility for my actions for the first time ever. I guess you could say I'm almost like born again or something like that."

Hillary smiled. "Well as long as you're not going to try to convert me I can respect that."

"What do we do now?"

Hillary put her hand on his and smiled. "Now you recover, and then when you are well enough we go home to our family. We may not always agree with one another, but we are stronger United rather than divided, and wherever things go from here we will go together as a family."

The two of them looked at the television where the inauguration of Joe Biden was taking place. There would be no public spectacle with large crowds because the virus was still raging and Washington was still in a state of martial law. But Biden would take the oath of office and be affirmed as the legitimate president of the United States, a peaceful transition of power taking place like it had been done for the past 2 1/2 centuries without interruption, and Hillary knew then that whatever troubles lay ahead that they could deal with them.

"And to quote a great man, a Republican, we shall not let the union by the people for the people perish from the earth, and with that I swear to uphold the Constitution and principles of the United States of America," Joe Biden said.

As Biden began walking away from the podium where he stood gunshots rang out and there was the sound of screams.

"Sic semper Tyrannis, I do this in the name of Q, long live Trump, president for life!" one of the Secret Service agents said as he stood over the body of Joe Biden before being promptly gunned down himself.

Hillary tightly squeezed Brock's hand and he squeezed back and together they both looked on in mutual horror as the newly inaugurated president of the United States was killed within moments of taking the oath of office.

Epilogue

President Harris was sworn into the office as America's first female president that very same evening once everything was deemed safe. She vowed that as her first act as President she would immediately continue with the trial of Donald Trump for treason against the United States of America.

The very next day several states loyal to Donald Trump dismissed the trial as illegitimate, and together they formed a Confederacy of states and declared secession from the union of the United States of America, and with that the second American Civil War had begun.

Bonus Stories
The Election Day Massacre

"I'm urging my supporters to go into the polls and watch very carefully, because that's what has to happen. I'm urging them to do it."

Arlen smiled as he looked at the image of Donald Trump on the TV. To him Donald Trump was a Savior, practically God on earth, sent here to liberate the white race from the slavery and oppression that they faced during the Obama administration.

Arlen turned off the television and went to address his militia. They were a group of white supremacists, proud boys and other far right groups who had all come together to decide what they were going to do about election day.

"Well you heard our president, our great leader, he wants us to make sure that the liberals don't take this election from him and steal it from him like we know they are going to try to do so that they can impose socialism on everyone," Arlen said.

"Are we going to go to the polls with our assault rifles to intimidate the liberals and the snowflakes," Carson asked as he raised his hand.

Arlen smiled. "I know that that was originally our plan when the president first gave us our orders. But I think that a stable genius like him knows that we are wise enough to read between the lines. When he said to go and watch the polls to make sure the liberals aren't committing voter fraud, I think that he knows that we would take it by our own initiative to do more than that. This isn't just about intimidating the liberals, we have to find some way to close the polls altogether."

"How are we going to close the polls?" Rourke asked as he raised his hand.

"The way I see it Biden is ahead in many areas and Virginia could end up going for him," Arlen said. "A lot of these election victories are very narrow, with just a couple of hundred votes making the difference between one state going red or blue. What I am suggesting is that we go and we go to the black part of town where most of the niggers are planning to cast their vote. If we show up with our guns and begin shooting them that's hundreds of people who will have their polling place closed and potentially hundreds or even thousands of people who won't vote in Biden leaning districts. It will also send a message to all the other members of the mud races out there. If they tried to vote we will stop them. We are not going to let them take over this country and wipe out the white race. We are not going to have another eight years of socialism like we did under Obama."

"You really think that we can pull this off?" Dustin asked.

Arlen nodded. "Sometimes you have to make sacrifices for your country. It's possible that we could get killed or injured or arrested, but I'm sure that once we ensure that Donald Trump is President and he gets his next term he will eventually find some way to make himself president for life. Once he doesn't have to worry about reelection ever again he will let us take over altogether. That is when the true revolution begins. I have no doubt that we will be pardoned, maybe even given the medal of freedom as true patriots who are willing to lay everything on the line to ensure that our great leader gets to continue making America great again."

"What are you proposing?" Carson asked.

"What I am proposing is that we communicate with various other cells and organize a series of mass shootings throughout the country at polling places that are likely to go for Biden. If we can intimidate enough of the liberals away from going to the polling places, and if we can do it early in the morning so that many of them hear about it and get fearful about the shootings and maybe think twice about going to vote. I think that if we can just get a couple of hundred people, or maybe even a couple of thousand people to think twice about voting, then we can ensure that the state goes for our dear leader, our glorious president Donald Trump. This is the revolution; this is how revolutions happen, people with guns taking history into their own hands. Because if we lose this election we know that the liberals are going to find some way to take our guns away from us and then it will be white genocide all around. This isn't just about an election; this is about our very survival at stake. If we're not willing to die for that now we will surely die for it later, so the decision is yours, and I urge you to make the right one."

Arlen and the members of his militia all agreed with him. This wasn't just going to be some type of voter intimidation tactic or a run-of-the-mill mass shooting, this was going to be a coordinated effort by several groups to save the state from going blue.

All of the members of his group started cheering and opening cans of beer and spraying them all around as they started loading up all of their weapons in anticipation for tomorrow's massacre.

"This is going to be an election day that nobody ever forgets," Arlen said as he stroked his gun and smiled.

George woke up that morning bright and early because he wanted to be there as soon as the polls opened. He knew that they had closed a lot of the polls in the African-American parts of town, a very clear form of voter actual real suppression, a way of discouraging his people from voting. But he wasn't going to be intimidated by that. If his parents and grandparents could have dealt with fire hoses and dogs being sicked on them during the civil rights marches of the 1960s, then he could deal with an extra-long line to vote as this election could decide the fate of the entire country.

George wasted no time in putting on his BlackLivesMatter T-shirt because he wanted to really make a statement and wanted everybody who saw him at the polls to know why he was there.

"Are you sure we want to wear these today?" Gloria said as she put on her own BlackLivesMatter T-shirt.

George nodded. "Maybe I'm provoking controversy but we have both been active in the movement and we are not going to hide it on the most important day. If Trump gets reelected we can kiss any chance of police reform goodbye. I owe it to my brother who was killed in a police shooting when he was fully innocent. This shit has got to stop."

"Do you really think that Biden is actually going to bring about substantial police reform?" Gloria asked scratching her head.

George shrugged his shoulders. "Honestly at this point I don't even know anymore. I just know that there is a chance that maybe he will, but if he doesn't, well I know that there is no chance of the other guy will, and that's enough for me. If Trump gets a second term this is only going to get worse. Soon we will have the military just marching through our towns and who knows if we will even have the right to protest. This could be the beginning of a new start for America or our full descent into fascism."

"I fully agree with you but I also feel really bad about today," Gloria said as she shook her head before hanging it down and held her hands in what looked like a form of prayer. "You know I didn't sleep last night at all, and whenever that happens, well you know I can't sleep before something bad happens. Before my mother died, before a natural disaster happens, before 9/11, before your brother died, the night before Donald Trump was elected."

"You still think that you have some type of psychic sense don't you?"

"I don't know if I have some type of psychic ability, but I just know that every time I have a difficulty sleeping, well not every time I have difficulty sleeping, but every time before a major event happens that is bad for this country, I just know that I don't sleep a single wink."

"We just have to stay positive, it's natural to be nervous before a major event like an election this important, but Biden has a huge lead, so we have to just pray that everything is going to turn out all right."

"But maybe it's not that, maybe it's something else altogether. Maybe Biden will win the election but Donald Trump will overturn the results of the election. Maybe it has nothing to do with the election itself. I just know that whenever I have this feeling it is never good."

George put his hand on her shoulder. "Look we don't know what's going to happen, none of us do. The only way we can ensure things get better though is to go out there and do what we have to do. We are going to vote this bastard out of office and we are going to do whatever is possible to try and convince the new guy to deliver on his promises for real and lasting change. This is no time to back down and to take the coward's way out."

Gloria nodded. "Well let's just hope so, I suppose we better get going then."

"Gentlemen today is the day, it's now or never, if any of you want to take the coward's way out it's time to go home to your mommies right now," Arlen said. "But trust me if we do not use our guns today we will not get the chance to use them tomorrow. We know that the minute Biden takes office that there will be mass confiscation of guns and that the police will be completely defunded and the country will descend into anarchy, with the illegals and the niggers and all the other degenerates free to do whatever they want in this country. So if you don't feel that you are up to it now is the time to bail out."

"Let's give them hell!" Carson said as he held up his gun as the rest of the militia began cheering.

They all began marching towards the polling place with their assault rifles out and their Trump shirts and MAGA hats clearly visible.

As George and Gloria stood in line and saw the militia members approaching Gloria swallowed deeply and began to get nervous.

"I don't like the looks of this George," Gloria said. "Maybe we should go home."

George shook his head. "I don't like the looks of it any more than you do, but you know that they are just here to intimidate us, if we walk away from this though they win. They think that if they show up in their Trump paraphernalia with their assault rifles out that we will get intimidated and we will go home. But I can tell from the looks of this crowd that they are not going to be so easily intimidated. We have been through worse over the decades, so I'm not going to let this stop me from exercising my long fought for right to vote."

"All you snowflake niggers in BlackLivesMatter and antifa terrorists go home!" Arlen said over a bullhorn. "This is your last chance to leave and stop trying to steal the election away from our only true president Donald J Trump."

Several people in the line started cursing at the militia members and shouting at them.

"Well don't say we didn't warn you, you had your chance, now you have to pay the penalty," Arlen said as he and the other members started firing their guns into the long line of people waiting to vote.

"Get down!" George said as he ducked down on the floor pulling Gloria with him and just narrowly avoiding being shot by the hail of gunfire in their direction.

"We have an active shooter!" someone started shouting. "We

have several active shooters."

George and Gloria began running with other members of the crowd as the sound of gunfire echoed through the air. Gloria continued running and that was when she noticed that George was no longer behind her.

"George, George where are you," Gloria said as she saw George on the floor. She ran over to him and cradled him in her arms. "George George George!" she shouted as she began sobbing.

"Go, get out of here!" George said as blood started coming out of his mouth. "I love you Gloria."

Gloria put down George's body, now no longer showing any signs of breathing, and she began running, barely able to breathe between hyperventilating and trying to catch her breath, tripping over another dead body as she continued running before picking herself up and continued running until she could no longer hear the sounds of gunfire.

Once she was a safe distance away she fell to her knees and broke down into hysterical sobbing as it became perfectly clear to her why she did not sleep last night and why she wouldn't be sleeping peacefully again for a very long time to come.

Gloria could barely think straight for the rest of that night but she forced herself to turn on the TV to watch the election results.

"And it looks like a clear win for Biden by a landslide," the announcer said on TV. "It looks like Virginia went blue."

Gloria once again broke into tears as she turned her hand into a fist and punched it into the palm of her other hand. "We did it George, it wasn't for nothing."

But as she told herself that the fact that her husband was now dead and lying in a morgue somewhere she couldn't honestly make herself believe that it had all been worth it. She continued watching the news report.

"But today's election is marred by tragedy where a mass shooting took place in a small African-American community where a group of white supremacists and militia members showed up with assault rifles and opened fire on a bunch of people waiting to vote," the newscaster say. "Dozens were killed and dozens more were injured and many are now on life support fighting for their lives, so we do not yet know the exact total of number of people who were killed. The overwhelming majority of the victims were African-American and the police ended up having to gun down most of the militia members. The one surviving member of the militia, apparently the leader, named Arlen, said that he did this to keep liberals from stealing the country from Donald Trump. He said he was they are to make sure that illegal votes wouldn't count and that he did it for the president who told him to watch the polls."

Gloria could feel herself digging into the palms of her hand till they drew blood. Her anger was so overwhelming that she couldn't even contain herself, she wanted to scream, she wanted to be sick.

"Before the results of the election came in Joe Biden had already gotten on an airplane and flown to the hospital to meet with survivors of today's tragic attack and we are trying to get a statement from him right now," the newscaster said as an image of Joe Biden at the hospital appeared on the screen.

"Mr. Biden did you hear the results of the election," the reporter asked.

Joe Biden looked up with tears streaming down his face.

"Who cares about the results right now," Joe Biden said as he looked at the bodies of several people on life support in the hospital. "Any electoral victory that started out marred by a tragedy like this can never be a cause for celebration."

As Gloria watched Joe Biden comforting the victims of the attack her anger momentarily dissolved as she understood what George was talking about, why this mattered. The nation was now in better hands, and if nothing else she knew that at least now we would have a president who actually cared, she just hoped that he cared enough to actually do something about it, and for the first time she felt confident that maybe he actually would.

"We are now getting reports that Donald Trump has given a statement," the reporter said.

Gloria now turned to the TV feeling her anger returning as the image of Donald Trump at his election headquarters appeared on the screen.

Another reporter was going up to Donald Trump. "Mr. President you have no doubt heard about the tragic events of today's mass shooting at a polling place in Virginia that is one of the largest mass shootings in American history, with the primary shooter saying that he did it inspired by your words to watch the polls and to intimidate voters, so you are being asked now, will you finally denounce their actions and denounce white supremacy once and for all."

Donald Trump stared out into the distance, looking like a zombie, looking like he was about to be sick, but Gloria knew in her heart of hearts he wasn't sick because of what had happened, he was sick because he knew that he had lost the election.

"I'm going to challenge the results," Donald Trump finally said, muttering incoherently as though he had just suffered a stroke.

"Mr. President that's not what I asked, I asked are you going to denounce white supremacy once and for all?" the reporter said as she shoved the microphone into his face but he continued just staring off into space with that thousand yard stare as though he had lost his mind. "Mr. President, Mr. President…" the reporter said as the president, as always, remained silent on the issue.

Gloria turned off the television, sat back in her chair, dug her fingernails into the fabric and finally let out the scream that she had been holding in all day.

<u>The Impeachment of President Trump</u>

Somewhere in the multi-verse in a universe parallel to ours that is slightly similar but in some ways different, there were a larger number of Republicans who had a conscience and decided to allow witnesses at the impeachment hearings of Donald J Trump. In this parallel world where Republicans still had a conscience they heard the testimony of the witnesses and they decided that they would move for impeachment of Donald Trump.

"This is a liberal plot against me!" Donald Trump fumed when he heard the results of his impeachment. "You are all traitors, traitors to me and to America!"

Parallel universe Donald Trump was completely furious. For the first time in his life he was made to be held to account for his actions. He realized he must really be living in some type of crazy parallel universe if someone such as him actually had to face consequences for a change.

"I just felt that we had to do what we had to do in order to save the integrity of the party," Mitt Romney said as Donald Trump threw his remote control at Mitt Romney's image on the television.

Donald Trump paced back and forth realizing full well that if the party had any integrity it would have never given him the nomination for the presidency in the first place. He didn't know how this could possibly happen but he had no intention of leaving office.

"I'll start some type of crisis so that they can't remove me from office," Donald Trump said as he thought that maybe there was some type of executive order he could use to nullify his impeachment. He figured that there were so many loopholes to impeachment that the people who wrote the Constitution never figured that a president would find some way to decide whether he could dismiss his own impeachment, but he figured that if anyone was good at evading the law he would find some way.

"My American people you have impeached me but I feel that you do not have the authority," Donald Trump said as he made a statement to the country. "That is why I encourage my followers to come to the White House and defend me and stop me from being removed from office."

Donald Trump felt confident that there was no way he could be removed from office but as he finished making his announcement that was when members of the military walked into the office ready to drag him from his position.

"What kind of bizarro world is this," Donald Trump said as he was forcefully escorted out of the Oval Office and dragged away.

Donald Trump then left office in disgrace saying that he had been wronged more than anyone in the history of the United States presidency. He got his own radio show and continued to rant and rave about how the decision was wrong and how the country would be begging to have him back in short order.

As president Pence took office as America's 46th president Donald Trump turned on his former vice president, saying that he was incompetent and that he couldn't manage the office of the presidency. Pence for his part said that God always make sure that wrongdoers are punished in the end.

As Donald Trump continued to rant and rave, now with nothing more to do but tweet all day and all night, the nation fell under a pandemic, and as president Pence mismanaged the pandemic to great degree Donald Trump said of how much better he would have done if he had been able to remain in office.

Eventually however Donald Trump came down with Covid, catching the very pandemic that he criticized Pence for mismanaging. As he became feverish and ill he started to hallucinate. He saw visions of another world, another world where people like him would never have to face consequences for their actions, where he was still in power and where he was the one overseeing this pandemic.

He ranted and raved in his delirium about how he had been wronged and how America was facing the consequences of removing him from office. He said that he felt in some type of other universe he was still the president, he said he could feel it, and he continued ranting about that, spouting off constantly as his delirium grew worse until one quietly he passed away with his last words being about this other reality that he had seen where he was still president and where everything was still right with the world in his opinion.

As the doctor pulled the sheet over Donald Trump's body he simply shook his head. "Whatever universe that is I am glad that we do not live in it."

Author Notes

I have written many dystopian stories that have been set in the near future but this has been by far the most near future speculative work that I have written, and I knew I wanted to write it right away and publish it immediately before any of the events in the book were set to pass. With any luck you by the time you are reading this it will remain just a work of fiction that doesn't remotely resemble reality. So consider this book to be a worst-case scenario of what could have potentially happened.

I was largely writing this novella more or less in real time. I originally conceived of this idea as a story late in August 2020 and I wrote the entire thing in the last week of September, where the events that I was describing in the first chapter were happening as I was writing them, and scary enough it seemed like as I was writing it the events that I was predicting were slowly becoming reality. Donald Trump had already been talking about how he wasn't going to accept the results of the election if he loses and then I thought that one thing that could have done that is if he got more power in the Supreme Court, and then tragically of course Ruth Bader Ginsburg dies, making this whole nightmare scenario much more plausible.

Never in American history in even the most partisan times or the most difficult times in our history have we ever had a president who frankly refused to leave office if he loses the election. The fact that he is discussing that as though it's an actual viable option and that more people haven't started rioting simply over that is in and of itself disturbing. For a sitting president to casually say that maybe he will just dismiss the election altogether because he doesn't like the result is the classic tactic of a dictator, and I have always believed from the very start the Donald Trump never aspired to be president, I always felt that he aspired to be dictator, and now it seems like he might actually make a bid for it to happen.

Hopefully in a scenario like this the military would actually bring about some type of military coup if it really came down to it to remove the president from office. But dictators throughout history have managed to overturn elections and overthrow democratically elected states time and time again in periods of crisis like the ones that we are in now. Although Donald Trump is an unpopular President, and at the time of this writing currently very far behind in the polls, among his supporters there is a fanatical base that really wants him to become dictator, that honestly does want him to become president for life, and that alone should be alarming to every American who is concerned about the fate of the future of our democracy, which has been slowly getting whittled away ever since 9/11.

The fact that I conceived of a novella like this and then it just starts coming true before my eyes and it actually becomes a possibility is of course the most frightening thing for any writer of a dystopian story. The whole purpose of a story like that is to warn people and hope that they do the right thing and make sure that it remains fiction. Writing it in real time as you see it playing out before your very eyes is the last thing that you really want to happen. A year from now I would hope that someone would read this and say that it was entertaining but a really far-fetched work of fiction and nothing more.

Even more disturbing is the prospect that there are white supremacist groups and militias throughout the country that do have a fanatical loyalty to Donald Trump and who might actually come to his aid and attempt to keep him in power. The fact that he has actually told groups like the proud boys to stand by and we will see what happens is quite frightening from any sitting president. Dictators don't need a majority of the population to accept them; they just need enough people to passively not resist them. The fact that Donald Trump is already starting to normalize in many people's minds the idea of dismissing an election or declaring it invalid makes it even more dangerous that he could actually convince his followers that it is the case, in spite of all evidence to the contrary. If we have ever had a president to lives in denial of reality it is certainly this one, and his followers are no different. They say you only need a few bad apples to spoil the bunch but you really only need a few bad apples to bring about hell on earth.

It is my hope that if Donald Trump did actually try to declare himself dictator as in this work of speculative fiction, that the people would, as in the story, rally against him and that they wouldn't just passively allow him to become dictator. I feel that the opposition and the resistance to him is strong enough that if he did try to become dictator the people probably would march on Washington, and we can only hope that the military would be marching with them. Hopefully any possibility of something like what happened in Germany in the 1930s and 40s happening here is only a slim possibility and that more people would refuse to go along with it.

However history has a way of repeating itself, particularly the bad parts of history, almost with a fair degree of near predictable regularity. I think if you told a person five years ago what America would look like in the year 2020 they would have said that we could have never gone this far in the direction of fascism that we have. Things like this don't happen overnight, it becomes normalized gradually and insidiously. Back in 2015 or 2016 nobody thought that Donald Trump would have a chance of becoming president. Everyone assumed that we would have found some way to have stopped him then and that he would have been rapidly impeached. However no tyrant comes to power on his own, with his allies in the government he has managed to evade consequences for his actions time and time again and gotten away with more and more. With vacancies opening on the Supreme Court and him strengthening his power literally anything is possible at this point. Five years ago the America of today would have seemed like a lunatic thing, it could never happen here people said, but it's happening, and it's happening right before our eyes. I am sure people in Germany in 1928 never thought then that in 5 years a fringe party like the Nazis would be running the country in 1933. If Donald Trump manages to remain in power I have no doubt that the America we will see in 2025 will probably be also beyond our imagining now, and certainly not for the better.

Originally when I started writing this novella I wasn't exactly sure where the main focus was. I wanted to focus on how Donald Trump maneuvered himself into the role of dictator but rather than being more of a political thriller I wanted it to be witnessed through the eyes of people living through it and how they reacted to it. So I thought a conflict between a brother and sister on total opposite sides of the political spectrum as they drift further and further apart was the best way to do it, as it would capture the polarizing nature of these times best, showing that some people would oppose a dictatorship but other people would be rallying to the cause, and that it could all take place in a very short time.

So ultimately I decided to go with a story about a brother and sister with the major events of the country sort of hanging in the background and influencing everything that was going on between them. Donald Trump only makes one direct appearance towards the end of the story before he is removed by power only at the last possible second once cooler heads realize that things have gone too far. So Donald Trump serves as more like the boogie man in the background influencing everything going on in the story, but having not a direct role in the story itself. It is more about the people affected by the events going on than it is more specifically about him, but those events drive everything in the lives of the main characters, so you see how they tried to go about living their lives as all these massive changes go about. Trump becoming dictator merely acts as a catalyst for the conflict between the brother and sister and their opposing ideas about what is happening, as no doubt is playing out among families all throughout the country right now and will continue to do so even further into the future.

I deliberately skipped over pretty much the entire month of October when I was writing this. I wrote the entire story in the last week of September, and I figured that I would jump forward to Halloween and the very end of October and then election day, with the main action being what happens after Donald Trump realizes that he's no longer going to become president and becomes more and more unhinged as he tries desperately to hold onto power. But October so far has been an interesting month. Many people have brought up the fact that before elections there is often an October surprise, with the first October surprise being Donald Trump, some might say with a degree of poetic justice, coming down with Covid through his own recklessness, something that was not really predicted and which did not factor into the story while I was writing it. And now as I am writing these notes we still have the majority of October left, so who knows what will happen. Like I said I wrote this largely in real time and it's very likely that by the time you are reading this the whole premise will hopefully be completely invalidated. This just represents an interesting glance at a worst-case possibility.

There was one influence on this novella that made it especially disturbing to me. I am a person who believes that we can see the future, or at least we can sense the future, usually only unconsciously. Back in 2004 I started writing a novel that I hopefully will finish one day involving the rise of a fascist dictatorship in the United States run by a billionaire sexual predator who eventually lead us into World War III and a nuclear Holocaust. It was started as commentary on the Bush administration, and I never thought that we would have anything worse than that, but once again it shows that humanity never learns and that it doesn't take that long for us to make the same mistakes again and again. Now that novel, which I still haven't finished, in retrospect seems prophetic.

I do not mean this book to be a prophecy but it was influenced by my own psychic experiences from many years back. I have been a practitioner of something known as remote viewing, where you get yourself in an altered state of consciousness and you can remotely view other times and places. Many years ago I tried getting general impressions about the future and as early as 2008 I got the strong sense that 2020 would be a monumentally historic year. I didn't see anything about the Covid epidemic, but I potentially felt that it was going to be a revolutionary year, perhaps the most historic year of my lifetime, and I thought that it mainly related to the fact that it was an election year, and I can say that whatever happens from this point on I was definitely correct about that.

However a more disturbing thing is that through my remote viewing I have often seen things that have later come to pass directly such as Hurricane Katrina and the London subway bombing of 2005 several weeks before they occurred. But back when I was doing these progressions to the potential future over a decade ago I did see one potential thing of what I felt was something like a new 9/11 that I felt took place in January 2020 or 2021, what looked like an explosion of a major building that I felt killed maybe upwards of 1000 people.

I should emphasize that while I have seen the future successfully through remote viewing the vast majority of things I have seen, including many other terrorist attacks, fortunately failed to come to pass. I feel these all represented only possible and highly changeable futures. But in light of everything that has happened recently I kind of wonder if I was picking up on something. I am starting to wonder if the tower or the building that I saw the came under terrorist attack was something like Trump Tower. Again it was totally a speculation of my part and in all probability this will end up being nothing more than one of many predictions of disaster and doom and gloom that hopefully fails to occur.

However I decided I definitely wanted to incorporate that into my novella as the terrorist attacks of January 11, 2021. Often throughout history there has been events such as the burning of the Reichstag or other single acts of terrorism that have justified mass sweeping powers, such as the patriot act passing after September 11. So the potential for something to go wrong at such a sensitive time in our history has never been more possible or probable. Let's just speculate for a moment that we have a president who loses election and doesn't want to leave office, in a nation that is polarized to the point where people are actively discussing the possibility of civil war, and then just one week before that president is supposed to leave office we face the most massive terrorist attack since 9/11. That's a monkey wrench thrown into things that could make anything happen. A dictatorship that seemed unlikely just the day before something like that happened could now seem very likely to the point where it is pretty much a foregone conclusion.

Again most likely this is nothing more than a work of speculative fiction, but in the few months before Donald Trump either leaves office or not, so many things can happen and history can change in a single instance, as anyone who has lived through 9/11 or the last two decades has seen. Could America actually go to Civil War? As unlikely as it sounds nothing could be ruled out at this point. Like I said earlier, five years ago any of this would have seen completely ludicrous, but now after the last five years anything is possible, literally anything, and often the worst possible of all worlds.

So can it happen here? You bet your ass it could! Will it? We can only hope not. But like with every event in history that is in the hands of the people living it and the decisions they make, and we can only hope that we make the right ones. But I have never been an optimist.

Now I will just say something about the bonus stories in this collection that I felt complement the main story nicely. The first story about a mass shooting occurring at a polling place on election day was actually a story that I conceived of back in February 2020. This was long before Donald Trump ominously told his supporters and his followers to watch the polls and intimidate voters. And we have seen time and time again in various acts of right-wing terrorism and mass shootings that many of the perpetrators have actively quoted Donald Trump or been inspired directly by his words. His refusal to condemn these people only inspires them further. The fact that the far right group known as the proud boys actually uses some of what he says as their new slogan is most telling of all.

So once again I hope that something like that doesn't happen, but the fact that since I had conceived of that idea but before I got around to writing it, that Donald Trump actively encouraged something along those lines, I just don't know. At this point once again anything is possible, so I hope that like with the rest of this novella that it proves to be just an imaginative worst-case scenario and that nothing remotely like this will happen. But again, is it possible? I have no doubt it is, and it is certainly just one more thing that we have to worry about. The fact that since I conceived of that idea that history has started moving in that direction and that such possibilities have actively been brought up and that people are actually talking about it as a possibility is enough to give anybody pause and a sense of unease.

The final story was one that was really short that I conceived of back when the impeachment hearings were occurring and after Donald Trump was impeached by the Democrats but didn't have enough votes from the Republicans to actively remove him from office. It was originally just going to be an alt history story about how things might play out if he had actually been impeached, and I thought that it just went along with the theme of this story of Donald Trump refusing to leave office. But then I decided to turn it into a parallel universe story where Donald Trump actually faces justice and imagines himself in our world where he never did. Like with everything else the final words of the doctor ring true, whatever universe we are living in it is not one that we would want to be living in. We are actively living in a dystopia.

So I hope you enjoyed this novella. I have many more Donald Trump stories that I hope to publish in the near future, nearly a half million words of them! I am going to be waiting until after the election to see what happens. With any luck Donald Trump will be leaving office and I can then publish all of those stories as a final fuck you to Trump as a time capsule of an era of insanity in American history that we can hopefully then leave far behind.

But if the worst-case happens in Donald Trump does become dictator all I can say is that, as a person whose social media postings got me a visit from the Secret Service, I will probably be among one of the first people to find myself in one of the extermination camps, and I can only hope that it's one of the nicer ones. And on that note of dark humor I leave you.

Stephen Sipila

10/12/20

You can read excerpts from my stories in my blog at https://stephensipila.wordpress.com/ and follow me on twitter at https://twitter.com/StephenSipila.

www.ingramcontent.com/pod-product-compliance
Lightning Source LLC
Chambersburg PA
CBHW071947120726
48001CB00005B/2072